MW01686439

Recipe for Love

An Andrade Christmas Novella

Ruth Cardello

Author Contact

website: RuthCardello.com

email: rcardello@ruthcardello.com

Facebook: Author Ruth Cardello

TikTok: tiktok.com/@author.ruthcardello

Bookbub: ruth-cardello

Before Abby met Dominic. Before Nicole and Stephan got back together. Confessed secrets drove Madison Andrade away from her family and into the arms of an arrogant, lusty Frenchman. All she wants for Christmas is a place to hide, but she cooks up much more than that in their short time together.

Richard D'Argenson is gaining fame for his talent in the kitchen, but he's missing the most important ingredient to any recipe—love.

Will he find it in the steamy night they spend together, and can what they share survive an Andrade Christmas invasion?

Copyright

Recipe for Love copyright 2014 by Ruth Cardello
Print Edition
ISBN: 978-1-963122-41-1

An original work of Ruth Cardello.

This book is a work of fiction. The names, characters, places, and incidents are products of the writer's imagination. Any resemblance to actual persons, places, events, business establishments or locales is entirely coincidental.

Cover art provided by Trevino Creative
www.trevinocreative.com

Acknowledgment

Thank you to my husband and family. Always better together.

Note to my readers

Recipe for Love is a novella that happens before both my *Legacy Collection* and my *Andrade Series*. It is a wonderful lead in to either. As the youngest of eleven children, I love the Andrade family. I hope you do, as well.

Award and Praise

New York Times and USA Today bestselling author

Praise for *Recipe for Love*:

"This is Ruth's finest work so far in my opinion. The thought she puts into the characters and the storyline are fantastic. Taking us into the life of Maddy and Richard was a wonderful feeling each of the emotional highs and lows of what they each were going through felt so real."

—Amazon Customer

"A down to earth read of family love and support. Richard a sexy Frenchman meets Maddy "princess," from each other they learn the true meaning of family."

—Amazon Customer

Chapter One

IF YOU HAVE to run away, run somewhere wonderful.

Madison Andrade paused to appreciate the beauty of the narrow, cobblestoned streets that paved this provincial town in southern France. Medieval stone arches accented the shaded passageway that ran between centuries-old buildings. The shops were decorated for the holiday season with garlands and lights. She stopped in front the boulangerie whose window boasted a festive display of many Galette des Rois, or Three Kings Cakes, adorned with gold paper crowns. If she had been visiting the area for any other reason, she would have purchased one, and then laughed with her friends or family as they each tried to find the hidden bean in the pastry that would award one of them the title of royalty for the day.

No parties on this trip.

Tucking her hands into the pockets of her double-breasted, red wool jacket, Maddy fought off a chill that had nothing to do with the cool temperature. One rebellious chestnut curl repeatedly escaped her attempts to pin it in her ponytail, flying wild and free in the wind.

A bit like me. A week ago she'd told the pilot of the private jet she'd received for college graduation, "Take me somewhere different, somewhere quiet where no one knows me." He'd chosen the Provence area around Sablet: a small village he said was famous for its local vineyards.

I don't drink wine.

But I guess that's okay, since I don't speak French either.

In true second-generation-American style, she barely even spoke Italian—a fact her parents, who made the trip back to the old country several times a year, lamented frequently. Her father, Alessandro, may have made a fortune in the technology industry, but he maintained a traditional home life. Her mother, Elise, was a warmhearted, pasta-loving woman with an easy laugh and quick wit. Along with her Uncle Vic, she had helped a large number of their family relocate to the United States, and the entire clan gathered frequently at their mansion near New York City.

It had been the perfect life, until she'd asked her father how he became so successful, and he'd told her a secret—a truth she couldn't accept.

"We should be heading to the airport," her six-foot-five wall of a limo driver, Gino, said in a tone that revealed his impatience with her decision to get out and walk the narrow roads. In his late forties, he'd been her driver and bodyguard since grade school. She didn't remember a time when he hadn't been by her side. "Your father told me to have you home by Christmas."

"I'm not going back," Maddy had snapped, then regretted the action. It wasn't fair to Gino to put him in the middle. It wasn't his fault she was crumbling on the inside. More softly, she said, "I can't." Just the thought of doing so filled her with a sudden nausea.

"You sound tired. Did you have breakfast?"

"Gino, I'm not a child."

He shrugged dismissively, just as her father would have, at the comment. Although they were not technically related, he was a second cousin twice removed, and that made him family. According to her father's definition, half of Italy fit those criteria. The Andrades were known for their generosity and loyalty. They took care of their own and the people who worked for them. Under their protection, widows didn't lose their homes. People got what they needed. Long-term employees became family, and, as her father always said, "To an Andrade, family is everything."

It was a beautiful philosophy—and at the end of the day, bullshit.

"You have to tell Stephan," she'd pleaded to her father.

"No," her father had said firmly, his belief that his brother had done nothing wrong obvious in the finality of his tone. Because he knew her too well, he'd warned, "And you won't either."

She'd grown up in a family of strong men, but her mother had always encouraged her to stand up for herself. In business, the Andrade men held positions of power and influence. In the home, her father would move heaven and earth to make his wife happy. And he was the same with his only daughter. At least he always had been, until they'd found themselves with distinctly different opinions of what was right. "You want me to lie?"

"I want you to say nothing."

"Then why tell me? Is this a test? Because it's one I'm going to fail. I can't sit back and watch Stephan live his life based on lies. I don't understand how you can."

"I see now that I shouldn't have told you the truth. Stephan was throwing his life away. Victor did what he felt he had to do."

"What if Stephan loved Nicole? What if he still does?"

"It's done, Maddy. Telling him now would only cause trouble in the family."

"Are you afraid he'll walk away if he finds out the truth? Andrade Global will no longer be important to him? Is this about money?"

Family is everything, unless they stand in the way of making a buck—then watch out.

Her father hadn't been one to raise his voice in his home, but in that moment he'd lost patience with her and had. "I love Stephan like he is my own son. He needed a reason to grow up, and Victor gave him one. The world is not a perfect place. People do what is necessary to protect their families. I don't judge Victor for the choice he made."

Toe to toe, father and daughter had glared at each other. "Of course not. You benefited from it."

"That's enough, Maddy. This conversation is over." Her father's face had held an angry red flush, yet he attempted to speak in a tone that would soothe her. "Your mother wanted to take you shopping with her today. You know how she likes to buy for all the children at the office. Go with her.

Perhaps it'll help you remember what's important."

"Money?"

With a sad shake of his head, he'd held her eyes before leaving, saying, "Family." He'd closed the door firmly.

Gino's questions pulled her back into the present. "What's bothering you, Maddy? Why are we here?"

The genuine concern in his voice made her wish she could tell him, but she couldn't. "I'd like to be alone, Gino. It's the middle of the day. This is a small town. No one knows who I am. It's safe."

"That's not your decision to make."

It should be.

From now on, it will be. "I am going for a walk by myself. I intend to have a quiet meal, alone, in one of these restaurants. I'll call you when I'm finished. There is no need to rush because I'm staying at the hotel again tonight."

"Your father—"

"Also needs to give me some space and he knows it. Call him if you want, but I already told him that I'm not going home yet. Not tomorrow, not for the holidays." *Maybe not ever.*

"*Mio trottolina*, you know how hurt he will be if you do this."

Like her father, Gino would never see her as more than a child, and it rankled her. "Trust me, the biggest gift I can give him is to stay away from him, from all of them." Meeting her protector's eyes squarely, Maddy spoke from her heart. "I know it's your job to keep me safe, but I need this. I need some time to think. I've spent my whole life following your advice without complaint—"

Gino's eyebrows rose to meet his hairline in disbelief.

"Most of the time," Maddy corrected. When Gino's expression did not change she added, "Come on, I've gotten better with age. I may have resented how you curtailed my social life in high school, but that's ancient history." She considered apologizing again, but decided it was better to focus on the present. "I'm twenty-three. If I want a few hours on my own, I should be able to have them."

After a long, assessing look, Gino nodded and put on his sunglasses. He said, "I'll be in the limo when you're ready. Call me if you need me." He gave the breast pocket of his dark suit a tap, referring to the cell phone she knew he kept there.

Maddy nodded and forced a grateful smile that seemed to reassure him. He turned and strode off, back down the way they'd come.

She hadn't made it very far when a light, cold rain started and she ducked into a small shop.

"Bonjour, mademoiselle," a petite woman called out from behind a small table. She was chicly dressed in a vintage Chanel tweed dress suit with a black braided trim that added a young playfulness to her otherwise austere profile.

"Bonjour," Maddy said with an apologetic smile. "I don't speak French."

The shopkeeper, who appeared to be in her mid-twenties, instantly switched to English. "No problem. Can I help you?"

Can you stop the questions that are swirling through my

head? Can you tell me what to do?

Tucking her errant curl behind her ear again, Maddy said, "I don't think so. I just needed a moment out of the rain." *And a moment out of my life.* She blinked back tears of confusion.

"*Mon Dieu*, you're wet. Well, you came into the right place. Plenty of dry clothes to choose from here." She called instructions across the shop to someone in the back room. Then, in English, she said, "Fran will make some coffee. You look like you could use some."

Looking around the shop quickly, Maddy saw the racks of retro clothing for the first time. Her mother would have loved the place. Although most of the family's clothing was tailor-made for them, she and her mother had spent many Saturdays hunting for rare vintage designer outfits. "Thank you, I would love some."

The woman cleared the table she'd been folding clothing on and covered it with a small white linen cloth. "Come, sit."

"Oh, you don't have to . . ." Maddy started to say, but the woman was already placing silverware and napkins beside plates.

"I don't have many chances to practice my English. Please."

Maddy placed her black Birkin bag on the floor and sank into one of the chairs offered, only then realizing how very tired she was. She hadn't slept well in the week since she'd last spoken to her father. Another young woman placed a fresh pot of coffee between them. "Thank you," Maddy said, gratefully accepting the steaming cup. She drank it black, barely feeling its burn.

The shopkeeper took the seat across from her. "My name is Alyson."

Maddy let the coffee cup warm her cold fingers. "Mine is Madison, but you can call me Maddy."

"Maddy. That's a beautiful name. You're American?"

"Yes. Is it that obvious?"

"Not jeans-and-tennis-shoes obvious, but I love your accent."

"Your English is very good."

The other woman smiled, and Maddy relaxed. For a few minutes they talked about the weather and the beauty of the town. Then, as if she'd been holding the question in for too long, Alyson asked, "Are you in some sort of trouble?"

"I'm sorry?"

"Your clothes are expensive, but you look exhausted and pale. Are you on the run from a wealthy lover?" When Maddy blushed, Alyson said, "I'm sorry. My imagination is over the top. I know. You don't have to tell me anything."

On the run from a wealthy lover? A tempting alternative to reality. Why be honest when no one else was? Maddy leaned forward and lowered her voice. "Please don't tell anyone that you saw me."

Alyson's eyes rounded. "You really are on the run?"

I wish I were. "Yes." A wicked thought came to her. She'd never deliberately done anything to worry or anger her parents. She'd happily followed their rules, secure in the belief that they loved her and would always keep her safe.

That was before she'd discovered how little she actually knew them.

Maybe it was time to show them how little they knew her.

And what their lie had cost them.

Maddy turned and looked at the racks of clothing and then back at Alyson. *I could disguise myself.* Urgently, she said, "I have money to pay you. Will you help me get away?"

Alyson reached across the table and took Maddy's hand in hers. "Women stick together, *non?* How can I help?"

Although Maddy felt a little guilty for not correcting Alyson on her situation, she'd already set herself on this course. "I need to disappear, but it won't be easy. I didn't come here alone."

"He's here?" Alyson whispered urgently.

"No, but my bodyguard is. I'm never allowed anywhere without him."

"Controlling bastard. No wonder you left him. I'll help you. Do you have anywhere to go?"

Maddy thought of all the homes her family owned and shook her head. No matter which she chose, which friend or family member she turned to, her father would know. With only a few hundred dollars in cash, her options were limited. Using her credit card would give her location away. There was a downside to coming from a family who'd made their fortune in technology.

"I would let you stay with me, but I have two roommates and it's not possible. However, my brother has a house just outside of town," Alyson said. "He has plenty of empty bedrooms and he is almost never there."

"I couldn't," Maddy said. It was one thing to agree to Alyson sneaking her out of town and another to impose on her family.

"He won't care. Trust me. You could be there a week and he wouldn't notice."

Mouth suddenly dry, Maddy asked, "Are you suggesting that we don't tell him?"

Alyson laughed. "Oh, I'll tell him. He just won't hear me. He's very intense, you know? All he cares about is his restaurant. He's a chef, quite a famous one locally. If you were a pistou or a macaron, he might notice you, but everything else is an annoyance, you understand?"

Not really, but Maddy imagined a short, stocky Frenchman in an apron and chef hat, and suddenly the thought of staying with him no longer seemed intimidating. "If you're sure it wouldn't be a problem . . ."

Alyson stood confidently and declared, "No problem at all. Do you have clothes with you, or will you need everything?"

"I—I guess I would need everything." *If I'm crazy enough to do this.* "I don't have a lot of cash on me, but I have some."

Alyson led her to one of the changing rooms and said, "Consider these a gift." She looked Maddy over to assess her size, then walked back to the racks and flipped a few articles of clothing over her arm.

"I couldn't possibly not pay you," Maddy protested and started to dig through her purse for money.

Alyson returned and laid a hand on her forearm to calm her. "You pay me when you can. It's not a problem. I trust you."

Although it was far from the first time Maddy had witnessed an act of charity, she had never been the recipient, and she wasn't quite sure how to handle it. *She's helping me because of a lie. I'm here because I can't stomach my parents' lie. I have to tell her the truth.* "You do not know me—" she started her confession, but Alyson spoke over her.

"I was you, once." The Frenchwoman's eyes misted over. "There must be something about this town, because I came here to this very shop, desperate and alone, and found exactly what I needed. The moment I saw you, I knew we had something in common and I want to—how do you say it—pay my good fortune forward?"

Because we're both scorned women on the run? Maddy felt trapped by her lie. She did want to escape—escape her family and the truth she wasn't sure she could keep from Stephan the next time she saw him. *Does it matter why I accept help as long as I need it?*

Desperate justifications were the first sign that you're doing something wrong. Unable to meet Alyson's eyes, Maddy accepted the clothing and said, "I haven't been entirely honest with you, but you should know . . ."

Alyson nudged Maddy into the changing room and closed the door between them. "It doesn't matter. You're free now."

Free. Maddy sighed and began to try on the clothing Alyson had given her. Each outfit fit as if it had been made for her, and their simplicity was refreshing. Alyson had a good eye for sizes and style. Although the clothing was from past seasons, the skinny jeans and high-heeled suede cutout boots Alyson had picked were still in fashion.

Dressed in jeans and a tucked-in oversized linen shirt, Maddy rejoined Alyson, whose arms were overflowing with two shirts, a skirt, and a pair of slacks. Alyson placed them in a large white plastic bag with handles. She accepted the articles of clothing Maddy had brought out with her and added them to the bag.

Maddy asked, "Are you sure I can't give you something for these now?"

"I'm sure," Alyson said. "I've included some intimate garments and a modest nightgown. You can't sleep naked at my brother's house. Although, then he just may notice you, *non?*" She winked and smiled.

"I'm sure your brother is wonderful, but even if he did like me, I'm not looking for a relationship right now. My life is already out of control."

Alyson studied Maddy for a moment, then nodded. "I understand that feeling, too. Come, let's go. I'll call my brother on the way. Don't worry. You don't have to like him. He's a big boy, *non?* He takes care of himself."

"Are you sure he'll be okay with me staying there?"

"*Oui, oui,* although he may say differently. The barking dog is not the one who will bite, you understand?"

Maddy shook her head as she followed Alyson out the shop's back door and into the small alley where her car was parked. "Not really, no. I'm not a dog person."

Alyson laughed as they both buckled themselves in. "I love American humor. You're so funny."

Maddy clung to the door handle as the small yellow Renault Clio hatchback flew down the narrow driveway and cut off another as it flew onto the main road. *What if Alyson really does know who I am, and I just became the most willing kidnappee on the planet? No one knows where I'm going.*

Am I standing up for myself and what I believe in, or putting myself in danger?

For once, I'm not sure I care either way.

✧ ✧ ✧

"GET OUT," RICHARD D'Argenson roared in French. The flurry of activity in the kitchen of his restaurant froze.

"Let me explain," the saucier answered hastily.

"There is no explanation needed. You rushed your sauce like a fumbling teenager chasing his first orgasm. People wait for a year to taste my specials. Do you think they want this . . . shit?"

"I just raised the heat a little to shorten the cooking time by a minute or so . . ."

"*Just . . . just . . .* if you wonder what holds you back from greatness, the answer can be found in that one word. Your job was to precisely follow my instructions. I create. I experiment. You take direction and learn. When you have your own restaurant you can serve them whatever slop you want, but here you cook the way I say or you go. So, get out—"

"You can't fire me with no notice and just before Christmas."

"That's not my problem."

"Please, I'll watch my times more carefully in the future . . ."

Richard's cell phone rang in his pants pocket. Everyone knew not to call him during busy hours unless it was a life-or-death situation, and even then he'd rather hear about the outcome later. He let it ring through to voicemail, but then it began to ring again.

"What am I going to tell my wife?"

"Mon Dieu!" Richard growled as he whipped out his phone and barked, "What?"

Unlike almost everyone else in his domain, his sister did not waver or apologize in the face of his temper. "Richard, I have a favor to ask."

"I'm busy right now," Richard snapped, pinning the man across from him with a glare. "If I don't get this idiot out of my kitchen soon, no one will eat tonight." His next threat was issued to the others who had paused to watch the exchange. "And no one besides me will be working here tomorrow."

All but the man he was firing returned to their stations and resumed cooking.

"Then just say yes," his sister suggested.

"To what? Say it fast. I don't have time for this nonsense."

"I need a place for my friend to stay for a few days."

"No. Absolutely not."

"Richard, this is important. I'd have her stay with me, but you know I can't. Please? You have so many rooms that just sit empty."

"I'm not a hotel."

"She has nowhere else to go. She's desperate."

"That's not my problem."

"Richard, have some compassion. She just broke up with a wealthy man and needs a place to disappear for a while. Do you remember Maman's second husband? These things can be tricky."

"This sounds like an equally tiresome situation."

"Do this for me, Richard. I promise, you won't even know she's there."

"That's what you said about the cat you brought me, and he's still at my house destroying my curtains."

"This is different. Trust me."

The man before him was still pleading for his job, but Richard had tuned him out.

"Fine. She can stay the weekend, but that's it. I won't be there very much anyway. This is a hectic time for me."

"Thank you, Richard. You won't regret this."

"I'd better not," he said and hung up.

The saucier said, "You're a reasonable man—"

"Is it reasonable to agree to house some crazy woman in my home and likely be robbed in exchange? *Non*, I don't think so. But I do it because it is the right thing to do. Just like giving you the opportunity to walk out of here on your own without the embarrassment of me throwing you out the door. I offer you a chance to retain your dignity." He looked down at his watch. "That offer expires in thirty seconds."

"I have said I won't do it again. What more do you want from me?"

"Twenty seconds. Please don't drag this out. I have a soufflé in the oven."

"You're insane."

"Ten seconds." Richard removed the cloth wrapped around his waist and said, "I'd hate to get blood on my favorite apron."

The man paled and retreated a few steps. He appealed to the sous-chef. "Bertrand, talk to him. Tomorrow is Christmas Eve, for God's sake."

The sous-chef, an older gentleman with white hair and an easy smile, intervened. "Richard, let me handle this. Thibeault, go back to your station. Finish your sauce, then go home. Come in tomorrow and we'll discuss if you still have a job."

Richard turned to the man he normally respected. "You forget your place, Bertrand. This is my kitchen."

When the saucier had returned to his station, Bertrand said, "Richard, I have worked with you for many years now, isn't that so?"

His temper cooling, Richard gave a reluctant nod. Once upon a time, Bertrand had taken a risk with Richard and given him the money he needed to open the restaurant. They were partners of sorts. Bertrand was a good chef, but he acknowledged Richard's gift, and that they worked better together when Richard created and Bertrand maintained.

"I know the holidays make you a little crazy in the head."

Bertrand smiled as he spoke. "Last week you would have bellowed and scared the man into precision. You wouldn't have fired him. Perhaps it is you who should take a day off. Go see your sister. Take the vacation you never allow yourself. Face the demon that makes this time of year unbearable for you."

"When I want your advice, I will ask for it," Richard growled.

"What kind of friend would I be if I waited that long?" Bertrand said cheerfully and walked away.

In the quiet that had fallen over his kitchen again, Richard roared to his staff, "Get back to work. We have people to feed."

With a nervous burst of energy, the kitchen returned to order and productivity.

Richard sighed with relief when he checked on his soufflé and saw that it had a minute or two left to firm. He hadn't ruined it yet. He caught the saucier watching him cautiously from across the room and swore under his breath. It was true: Any other week of the year he would have chastised the man for his lack of dedication to detail, but he wouldn't have fired him for the first offense. In that, Bertrand was right. He was wrong, though, to think that taking a day off would lighten the dark mood that descended on Richard each Christmas.

In Sablet, celebrations started before Christmas and lasted well past. He wasted time each year decorating his restaurant for a holiday that meant nothing to him and fending off invitations from neighbors who thought a simple date on the calendar meant he should not be alone—unable to believe that alone was how he preferred to be.

Alone was never a disappointment. The days when he tried to please others, like his sister, by joining in festivities were long gone. She still dropped by on Christmas morning, but she had friends in town who had become her family, and after a brief visit she would leave to celebrate with them.

And leave him in peace.

Something he wasn't going to have now that he'd agreed to Alyson's ridiculous request.

What the hell was he going to do with a woman in his house for Christmas?

Chapter Two

LATER IN THE evening, Maddy was exploring the west wing of a ten-bedroom stone mansion and wondering about the man who owned it. Moderately expensive paintings were scattered throughout the house, alongside vacant spots where others had likely hung.

What had happened to them?

The furniture was elegant in design but told the same story as the empty places on the walls. Each room contained just enough furniture to be functional, but the settings where valuable pieces might have been showcased were bare.

One day before Christmas Eve and there wasn't a ribbon, candle, or wreath in sight. Curiosity drove her through each room as she hunted for even the tiniest evidence of holiday cheer. She thought of the lengths her family went to each year to decorate their thirty-plus-acre estate near New York City. There wasn't a corner of the house that didn't sparkle cheerfully or display photos of past Christmases. She and her mother spent an entire day each year directing the staff on exactly how and where to hang the festive greenery. It was something she'd often taken for granted.

The stark absence of any seasonal decoration saddened Maddy on many levels. She felt sorry for the man who owned this large, cold house. Had he experienced a financial devastation that had taken away not only his treasures but also his ability to enjoy his home? The bedrooms she entered were clean and well maintained, but each was as lifeless as the last. If one was his, she couldn't tell it apart from the others.

Maddy headed back to the suite Alyson had helped her settle into and felt a bit ridiculous. *What was I thinking? I have money. I don't have to hide out here. I should call a car service and check into the nearest hotel.*

But then my family will know where I am.

She'd turned off her phone on the drive over, right after sending her father a text: "Tell Gino I won't be meeting him at the limo. I'm okay." Short. To the point. Let them know she was alive without giving away her location.

She sat on a couch near a large double window and smiled when the cat Alyson had called Minet hopped into her lap. She petted him absently while talking herself through her decision. "They should be grateful. I'd never make it through a family dinner and keep my silence."

The cat's only answer was a happy purr. Maddy picked him up and looked into his golden eyes. "What story did you use to get here?" The cat blandly looked back at her. "I supposedly am on the run from some ex-lover. What a joke. Who can date with Gino around?"

The cat mewed loudly. Maddy joked, "Neutered, huh? Okay, you win. Your love life officially sucks more than mine."

Putting Minet at her feet, Maddy stood again and decided to change into something for sleep. As she hunted through the top layers of clothing Alyson had bagged for her, she said, "So, tell me about the man who owns this house. What does he look like? Is he short? Does he sample too many of his desserts? How about his teeth? Does he have any?"

Finally her fingers touched something silky. Maddy pulled the silky nightgown out and held it up. Although it was long enough to almost reach her knees, the material was thin to the point of practically being sheer. Pink silk with accents of white. Apparently she and Alyson didn't share the same definition of *modest*. The pink thong underwear that came with it still had a tag on it. No surprise. Does underwear matter when it's also see-through?

She debated discarding the nightgown and sleeping in her slacks. But Alyson had told her she might not even meet Richard. He closed his restaurant late and opened it early. He was okay with her staying there for the weekend as long as he didn't have to see her. A bit eccentric, but his house was certainly large enough to allow for such an arrangement.

And his lack of interest in his houseguest made her choice of sleepwear irrelevant. Maddy held the pink nightgown up again. It really was beautiful, and her clothing was damp from the rain. She didn't plan to leave the suite that night. Giving in to impulse, she stripped and put on the delicately made lingerie. She took a blanket from the bedroom, dug her tablet out of her purse, and took both with her to the couch. Nothing else in her life was as she'd thought it would be, but rereading one of her favorite romances was soothing and provided a temporary escape from the reality that had sent her into a tailspin.

Minet curled up on her feet, purring loudly. Maddy closed her eyes, lulled by the rhythmic sound, and didn't notice when she dropped her tablet to one side. The story on the page continued like a movie in her dream. A wondrous passionate scene where all of her wanton desires were being fulfilled by a beefy, broody cowboy.

✧ ✧ ✧

TIRED AND IRRITATED with himself for having agreed to a put up a guest for the weekend, Richard entered his mansion. The lack of lighting inside gave him hope. There was a chance his sister had come to her senses and taken her friend where she belonged: a hotel. Or back to her ex-lover. Anywhere but his house.

He should have never agreed to it, but the mention of his mother and her previous states of desperation had been enough to confuse a yes out of him.

The cat he'd never named, because he still had no intention of keeping it even though it had lived with him for a year, did not meet him at the door as it normally did. It didn't twirl around his legs, half tripping him, as he made his way to hang up his coat. Nor did it run up the staircase ahead of him in a wild attempt to beat him to his bedroom, hoping it would be allowed to claim a lower corner of the bed if it got there first.

No, the cat was strangely absent, which meant that someone else might indeed be present. Richard opened the door to a guest suite in his home. There on the couch, curled on her side beneath a solid blue comforter, lay his unwanted guest, sleeping peacefully. He stepped closer. Her chestnut curls were loose and cascaded around her, looking so soft he had to fight the urge to touch them.

She moaned softly in her sleep and shifted, revealing only the slightest hint of what filled her dreams. Her lips parted slightly and she moaned again, making Richard's heart beat rapidly.

He knew he should walk away and leave her to her dreams, but he couldn't. He stood over her, wondering what color her eyes were, and if her body matched the beauty of her face. It probably did. When a woman decided to trade her self-respect for the comforts a rich man could provide her, staying trim was often an unspoken part of the deal. His mother was both beautiful and physically fit. She had to be or she wouldn't be able to lure men, one after another, into marriages with lucrative prenuptials. If his mother cared as much about her family as she did about landing her next husband, he might talk to her more than once a year. For now, a brief phone conversation every twelve months was all he could stomach.

Regardless of how innocent the woman before him appeared, he knew the truth about her, and that was enough to counter the temptation of her perfect features. It was no surprise that she'd talked his sister into depositing her at his house—a woman like her would always be on the prowl for another man to support her. He wondered if he should tell her that most of his money was tied up in his restaurant and the mansion he'd never been able to part with.

No diamond necklaces here, ma puce. *Sorry to have wasted your time.*

The cat raised itself from its curled position at her feet, then lowered its head and dug its claws into her ankles. She partially woke with a start and swatted one hand at the air above the cat, then seemed to come more to her senses, groggily pulling the cat to her chest in apology. "Oh, it's you. For a minute there I thought you were—I don't know what I thought, but you should be a more careful kitty when you're waking someone up. I'm still jumpy."

American. Just my luck. His restaurant filled with them around the holidays. *Why not in my home, too?* "My fault," Richard said dryly in English.

Her eyes flew to his and, before he could say more, she screamed at such a high volume that he was grateful his neighbors lived acres away or they surely would have called the police. She clutched the cat to her chest with such force that it also screeched.

He stepped closer to intervene, fearing the cat would turn and claw the poor woman. His quick approach elicited a second scream from the woman. *"Arrête,"* he ordered impatiently and seized the cat. "You're scaring him."

Red-faced, the woman scrambled to stand and reprimanded him. "Then stop scaring *me.*"

With the now-calm cat tucked beneath one arm, Richard said coldly, "I was merely coming in to check on my houseguest." He stressed the last word, making his feelings about having her there quite clear.

She stepped forward and her jaw dropped open. "You're Alyson's brother?"

"You were expecting someone else?"

"No, I just thought you'd be—" She didn't finish the sentence. Instead, she gave him one more appreciative once-over, then blushed. "Shorter," she finished, then blushed again.

Appreciative looks from a woman were something he normally enjoyed, but hers lit a fire within him so intense that it shook him. The lamp behind her illuminated her gown in such a way that it became mostly transparent, and his heart began to beat double time in his chest. Her long brown curls ended just short of the tips of her beautiful breasts, which were now quite visible to him. Small and pert, just as he liked them. He forced himself to raise his focus to her face and reeled beneath a second punch of attraction when their eyes met.

Those eyes—*mon Dieu*, how they completed the package: dark and rich like a fine chocolate and flashing with temper. She was easily the most beautiful woman he'd ever seen. And probably the most dangerous. Women like her knew how to use their beauty to manipulate.

In what was likely a false show of modesty, she looked down at herself, gasped, and hastily wrapped herself in the comforter. She looked up at him from beneath her long lashes and said, "I'm sorry I screamed, but I've never done anything like this before."

Really? He doubted that. "I'd think a woman like you would be used to waking up in a great many unusual places." The words burst from him angrily before he could consider what he was saying.

Pink spread up her neck and cheeks. She hugged the blanket tighter around her. "Well, that's rude and uncalled for. Your sister said you were fine with me staying here. If that's not the case, all you have to do is say so." She turned away from him, then spun back and advanced a few steps. "But who are you to judge me, anyway? Even if I've slept with a hundred men—or half of France for that matter—how would that affect you? All you know is that I needed a place to stay and your sister brought me here. I could be running from the most horrific experience, in which case you'd be demeaning an already tormented woman. Which one of us should be ashamed?"

Her passionate speech sent flames of desire through him. Right, wrong, guilty, or innocent: He no longer cared. He didn't want to be attracted to her, but he was. He closed the distance between them and leaned down until his lips almost touched hers, testing. Her lips parted and her hot breath mixed with his. He knew he should tell her to leave. He didn't want or need a woman like her in his life. But his thoughts remained unspoken, and the air between them sizzled with sexual tension unlike anything he'd ever felt before. "What's your name?"

Seemingly as mesmerized by him as he was by her, she murmured, "Madison. My friends call me Maddy."

He rolled her name over his tongue. "Madison. No last

name?" Insane as it felt, he wanted—no, needed—to know more about her. He needed to test the attraction between them, pull her to him, see her eyes light with a fire just for him. He was a passionate man and one who was not ashamed of his fondness for women. Most women. Not ones who collected men like some collect shoes, discarding them when they came across something better.

He knew better than to get involved with a woman like that.

But he couldn't step away.

She met his eyes, looking like she wanted to give herself to him, even as she denied him with her words. "Not one that you need to know. Especially since it looks like I'll be leaving tonight."

He ran a finger lightly down one side of her neck, tracing the wild pulse there. "You don't have to. I may be able to help you."

"Really?" she asked breathlessly.

He gave her a lusty grin. "Yes. If your goal is to claim that you've slept with all of France, who am I to stand in your way?"

Her cheeks reddened and she raised an impulsive hand toward his face. He caught it easily and simply held it to one side. He was toying with her, and they both knew it. Her temper excited him. Was she as impulsive in bed? He was sorely tempted to find out. "Why so angry? I'm no longer judging you. In fact, I applaud your—enthusiasm."

"You're a real jerk," she said, attempting—but failing—to pull her hand free from his.

"I've been called worse—tonight, in fact."

"Let go of my hand."

He brought it to his lips and kissed the inside of her wrist before releasing it. "You intrigue me. Outraged virgin or high-paid whore? You'd have me believe that you're fearful and on the run from someone, yet you claim my home with the arrogance of someone who is used to getting what she wants. I tell myself it doesn't matter, but I've always enjoyed a good puzzle." He tugged on the sides of her large wrap and pulled her forward, flush against him. "I've never liked being given a recipe. I prefer to taste the food, let it fill my senses, and discover each ingredient myself. Then and only then is it mine to experiment with." He brought his lips down close to hers again and flicked his tongue over her bottom lip in invitation. "Let me taste you, Madison. I promise, I will make sure your pleasure surpasses my own."

She put a hand on his chest as if to push him away, but it merely rested between them over his wildly beating heart, while shook her head as if trying to clear it. "I may have given you the wrong impression."

Following his instincts, he licked the exposed curve of her neck and felt her shudder with pleasure against him. Desire for her swept away the last of his resolve. He was a man who believed in following his passions. And tonight, there was only this one woman and his need for her. "I don't care about why you're here. All I care about is this." He claimed her mouth with all the passion building within him and loved how her tongue met his eagerly.

✧ ✧ ✧

HOLY MOLY.

Nothing in Madison's sexual past had prepared her for the instant attraction she'd felt when Richard had stepped out of the darkness. A few inches over six feet with a deliciously muscled body, he was definitely not what she'd been expecting. Now, moments after meeting him, she was kissing him more intimately than she'd ever kissed one of her boyfriends. His hands cupped her buttocks and held her firmly against him. She should be afraid. *Throw-all-decorum-to-the-wind lust doesn't happen outside of the movies, does it? And if it does, you should at least know the other person. So this is what happens when you wear see-through thongs.*

So much for him not noticing I'm here.

Maddy's desire surged. She arched backward to allow him access to her shoulder. Nothing mattered except the heat that was spreading through her and the need to be closer to him. He trailed kisses across her exposed collarbone and she arched even farther back, desperately wanting to feel those hot kisses farther down. Her nipples tightened and begged for his attention.

I'm not the kind of woman who has a one-night stand.

Any stand, for that matter.

Maddy shivered with desire when Richard cupped one of her breasts in his hand. His thumb caressed and teased. His breath warmed her as his mouth replaced his hand. He suckled her, his hot, wet tongue circling her. She felt the gentle tug all the way down through her stomach. Her body readied itself for him, pulsing and tingling.

How can a bad idea feel so good? Every place he touched burned for him. Every place he didn't yearned for him. *I should stop now before this gets out of control.*

If it's not already.

As if he could hear her inner debate, Richard raised his head. His eyes were ablaze with desire for her, but his voice was soft. "What is it?"

What is it not? I've left everything I know behind to shack up with a stranger and, instead of locking my door and seeking a way to make a dangerous choice safer, I'm seriously considering throwing my moral compass in the trash.

"I'm a virgin," she blurted.

He gripped her by both upper arms and demanded, "A what?"

Embarrassment flooded in and she tried to pull away from him. "You heard me."

Richard's hands tightened on her arms painfully. "Are you joking?"

I wish I were.

Richard bent, lifted the blanket off the floor, and tossed it at her. He was saying something angrily in French, and for once she wished she'd paid attention to her language tutors. *Although when they said I'd need the skill someday, I'm sure they never imagined this scenario.* "A minute ago you didn't care who I'd slept with. Why does it matter if I haven't been with anyone?"

Have I lost my mind? Am I actually arguing for him to continue pawing me?

He paced in front of her, running his hands through his hair and cursing in French. She had no problem translating most of that. Some profanity is universal. He grabbed her by an arm again and swung her to face him. "I don't sleep with virgins."

"Fine," she said and wanted to kick herself for sounding less and less mature with every word that came out of her mouth. She tried, unsuccessfully, to pull her arm free from him.

He stood in front of her, close enough that she had to tip her head back to meet his angry glare with one of her own. "What about your *lover*? Did he expect something in return for supporting you? Is that why you left him?"

Still feeling a bit raw from his refusal, Maddy snapped, "This isn't about a man."

"So, you lied to my sister?"

Oh, yeah, that. "She assumed that was why I looked upset. I just didn't correct her." *Because apparently lying runs in my family.*

"Are you in trouble with the law?"

Maddy almost laughed, until she realized he wasn't kidding. "No, but I needed to find someplace where I could think."

"And you thought you could do that here?"

She raised her chin defiantly. "You were supposed to be short and fat."

A corner of his mouth lifted, as if her comment amused him despite his annoyance. As he continued to look at her, his expression changed, and with unexpected compassion he asked, "Did someone hurt you?"

The question threw her. They had, but not in the way she knew he thought. It was too complicated, and the details could potentially hurt her family if they went public, so she merely shook her head.

He didn't believe her. He rubbed a hand roughly over his face as if trying to clear his thoughts. "You don't have to lie to me. You're safe here."

"Am I?" she asked hoarsely. They both knew what she was asking.

With his features set in harsh, cold lines, he said, "It was a kiss. People do more on the dance floor after a few drinks."

Where do you dance? Maddy thought as a gurgle of nervous laughter bubbled in her throat. "I should probably still go."

"I told you you're safe here. Nothing further is going to happen between us."

"Because I'm a virgin?"

He growled something in French beneath his breath. "*Oui*, and too young for me."

Let it go, the voice of reason in her pleaded, but she couldn't. "You're not much older than I am."

"In years, perhaps not. In experience, we couldn't be more different. Sex to me is like a good meal, pleasant but not necessarily best always served from the same cook. Could you handle that?"

"No."

"That, *ma puce*, is why you are perfectly safe here tonight." He turned and headed toward the door of the suite.

Maddy doubted that, after he'd walked out, she'd ever see him again. Despite their verbal clashes, the thought made her a bit sad. *What do you say to someone who just made a decision you should have—one you would have if you weren't so angry with the world that a dose of danger felt good?* "Richard," she called out to him softly, and he stopped. "Thank you."

He turned slowly and leaned against the doorjamb, watching her cautiously, "It's not a problem." Then he smiled a bit playfully and, in a beautifully sexy French drawl, said, "Well, it was less a problem before I saw those beautiful breasts of yours. But it's nothing a cold shower won't fix."

The connection they'd felt earlier deepened when she smiled at his joke and he smiled back. There was more intimacy in that moment than there'd been in kissing and ripping at each other's clothing. It shook Maddy. She didn't want him to leave, but she wasn't brave enough to ask him to stay. "I should have been honest with your sister. I'm here because I quarreled with my father. Have you ever been put in a situation where you have to do something, but no matter what you do, you know nothing will ever be the same?"

His expression darkened with the pain of some memory. "*Oui.*"

"What did you do?" she asked in a hushed tone.

"What I had to, and then I walked away."

"I don't think I can do that."

The sincerity in her voice seemed to touch a cord in him. He straightened from the wall and said, "It looks like you already did."

"I'm so confused," she admitted hoarsely.

He closed the distance between them and kissed her gently on one cheek. "You and I both, *ma puce*, I will not sleep easily tonight."

He spun and left with the cat following at his heels.

Maddy groaned and, picking up her tablet, walked alone into the guest bedroom. She slid under the covers of the bed, still clutching the device, which she didn't turn on. *I doubt there is a book on there that could make me forget that I almost gave my virginity to the first sexy Frenchman I met, only to be refused like I'd offered him a case of the measles.* She set the tablet on the night table, flipped the light off, and stared at the dark ceiling above. *Is he lying in his bed imagining what it would have been like between us? Not that I want to be just another meal he enjoyed and then forgot.* She closed her eyes and remembered how her body had responded to his touch. Her skin still tingled at the memory.

Sex is supposed mean something.

A hot night with a complete stranger would have been wrong.

She rolled onto her side and hugged one of the pillows to her chest.

Or it would have been heaven.

Chapter Three

EARLY THE NEXT evening, Richard paused from issuing orders to his kitchen staff to throw a sheet pan in the dish pit with enough force that the sound echoed throughout the room and caused a momentary halt in activity. With a glare, he set his workers back on task. They knew better than to joke with him when he was in a mood.

Yes, he held them to impossibly high standards, but he didn't ask them to give any more than he gave of himself each day: everything.

He was an artist, not a cook. He fed people's souls, the same way a painter or musician would. The world could survive without art or gourmet food, but who would want to live in such a world? He was driven to create dishes that would be remembered long after they were experienced. It was an obsession—until today.

The only thing worse than spending the day distracted by the thought of Madison in his house was the thought that she might no longer be there.

Memories of her tight body outlined by the light of a side lamp brought him to an uncomfortable level of arousal.

And those eyes. *Mon Dieu*, those chocolate eyes—flashing with anger, melting with desire, while she offered herself to him.

An offer I turned down.

No matter how he tried, he couldn't stop his thoughts from returning to his houseguest and their short encounter. He'd formed an opinion of her before they'd met and had been set to dislike her. Instead, he found himself fascinated, and not just sexually.

She was in his thoughts, his blood, an itch that could not be denied.

And all I did was kiss her.

I don't even know her last name.

If she left, I'd never be able to find her.

That thought was enough to have him striding over to Bertrand. Even though the restaurant was closing early that day, he couldn't wait a moment longer. "I'll be at my house if you need me, but only call if you've lit the place on fire."

His sous-chef was so surprised that he asked a question he already knew the answer to. "Y-you're leaving?"

Richard imagined Madison as he'd found her, lying on the couch, and hastily discarded his chef coat. Bertrand was perfectly capable of running the kitchen—even if it was the first time he'd been asked to do so. Richard had never been one to second-guess his decisions and was not about to start now. "I am."

"Are you ill?" Bertrand asked with real concern.

"No. I have something at my house that requires my attention."

Bertrand shook his head in confusion and said, "In all the years we've worked together, I've never seen you leave early. You don't celebrate the holidays. Is it your sister? Is Alyson okay?"

"Everyone is fine," Richard said impatiently. "I just have to go."

Bertrand persisted, "You know, we're business partners, but we're also friends. If you need help, let me know."

"I probably need psychiatric help, but tonight just worry about the restaurant."

A slow, understanding smile spread across the older man's face. "Only a woman could make a man that crazy."

"Just close the restaurant tonight. I'll be back tomorrow."

"Or not," Bertrand said happily. "Take your time. I'm perfectly capable of running this place without you for a few days."

Richard opened his mouth to say he'd be back early in the morning as usual, but if everything worked out the way he wanted it to, he wasn't sure he would be. So he kept his thoughts to himself and headed toward the door. Bertrand clapped his hands loudly and, in a tone much like Richard would have used, put the kitchen staff back on task.

Richard exceeded the speed limit on all the roads that separated him from the woman he couldn't stop thinking about. On the way he rehearsed how he would tell Madison that he'd changed his stance on virginity.

✧ ✧ ✧

RIGHT, LEFT, THEN another left after the farmhouse. Or was it left, right, then left at the farmhouse? Shit. Maddy stood at an intersection, wishing she'd paid more attention on the way into the small town near Richard's house. Her arms were aching from the weight of the bags she'd filled with Christmas decorations.

When she'd decided to head into town and pick up a few holiday items to surprise Richard, it had seemed like a good idea. However, getting lost outside the town near his house added an almost comically ridiculous element to the day.

Would it kill this town to have a taxi service? Not that it would have helped much because I can't remember his exact address.

Yes, please drop me off at the large stone mansion on the hill. Oh, all the mansions in this area are stone and seem to be on hills? Well then, how about the one owned by a hot French chef? There can't be many like him around.

Name? Richard.

Last name? Oh, I forgot to ask. Sure, I almost slept with him without that knowledge, but it would be helpful to know it now.

Or even the name of his restaurant.

No wonder Gino thinks I can't survive on my own. I feel like a five-year-old who should have worn a tag to help people return her home if she got lost.

Home.

Maybe that's where I belong. Maybe my father is right. Maybe if I grow up I'll understand why my family made the decisions it did.

I should call Gino and tell him to pick me up. Hard to ever truly be lost in the world of technology and GPS tracking. The moment I turn on my cell phone he'll find me. He's probably still in the local area looking for me. He'd never leave me. That used to make me feel safe. Now I feel cornered.

Choosing a direction, Maddy set off walking down a side road, regretting again that she wasn't wearing practical walking shoes. Her suede high heels were comfortable for a short stroll, but this was becoming a several-mile hike. She was dressed in black corduroy pants, an ivory loose-fitting sweater, and her jacket, and yet the wind blew right through the layers and chilled her skin. Along with the fading sunshine, the temperature was quickly dropping.

Nothing looked familiar, and her frustration was growing. At any other time in her life, she would have called her mother for advice, but she'd made that option impossible. She saw now that she should have spoken to her mother before leaving, but she'd been angry, and the anger had made her impulsive. Her mother must have known about Uncle Vic's lie. She'd probably known for years and done nothing. Maddy had always thought that she and her mother told each other everything. She'd been wrong.

Is that why I felt ready to toss my virginity to the wind? Do I want to hurt my family like they hurt me?

She remembered the feeling of Richard's lips on her body and blushed as her skin tingled in memory. *No, it was more than that.*

Although she was uncertain about how to deal with her family, she knew exactly why she was waiting for Richard to come home. *I've never felt anything like what I felt last night, I want to feel that again. I have to know if his kisses really are as good as I thought they were. Was my heart beating wildly the whole time we spoke because he'd woken me with a start or because our attraction was that strong?*

What would have happened if I hadn't blurted out my lack of experience? Does it matter? Will I ever find out?

The street ended in a driveway. Maddy cursed and waved a hand angrily at the waning late-day sun. She dropped the bags at her feet, hugged her thin coat to her, and shivered. As the sun slipped below the tree line she took out her phone and turned it on. She didn't need to call Gino. She'd known him long enough to be certain that he'd stayed nearby and would be there soon.

As she walked, she grumbled toward the sky, "You win. This was ridiculous from the beginning. It's time to go home."

Chapter Four

SHE'S GONE!

He'd known the moment he'd opened the door and been greeted by his lonely feline. He searched every room of his home even calling out her name a few times.

Gone.

He stood in the middle of the empty guest room and closed his eyes. It was for the best. He knew nothing about her outside of the innocence she claimed to have. Everything else had been a lie. For all he knew, her virginity could be a lie as well. Normally he wouldn't have agreed to house her in the first place. Alyson had caught him in a moment when agreeing had been easier than questioning. He should be relieved.

He looked around the room one last time and something caught his attention. A bag from his sister's store was on a chair. He searched it and realized it was clothing.

If Madison had left for good, wouldn't she have taken that with her?

Maybe. Maybe not.

Was it possible she had gone outside for a walk? No sign

of her anywhere.

He absently lifted his jacket off the rack near the back door and headed outside. Putting aside the questions raging within him, he called for her and continued his search. The sun was just setting over the tops of the trees. The evening air was cooling quickly.

He got into his car and started it, but he didn't put it in gear at first. *What am I thinking? That she's walking the streets like a lost child? Looking for her is likely a waste of my time. She's probably flying back to the States or in town flashing those big brown eyes at someone—offering another man what I'd declined last night.* Yet he threw his car in reverse anyway and sped down the driveway.

He caught a glimpse of a woman walking down a side road with shopping bags in each hand. He turned his car around with a squeal of the tires. In half a heartbeat, he'd pulled up next to her, jumped out of the car, and stood beside her. She shivered, and he swore. He took off his jacket and wrapped it around her shoulders. "Are you completely lacking in sense? It gets cold, even here in the South," he snapped, retaining his grip on the front of his jacket, effectively holding her in place before him.

The welcoming smile she'd flashed when she first saw him disappeared. "I was about to thank you for coming to find me, but I'll hold out for an apology first," she said, folding her arms before her, her chin set at a stubborn angle.

How prim and proper she sounded as she chastised him. He wanted to shake her as much as he wanted to kiss her. Well, not quite as much. "And what exactly am I supposed to apologize for?" He knew his tone was harsh, but he was angry.

She bristled defensively. "I didn't mean to get lost, and I don't deserve your snide comments. If you can't be nice, take your damn coat back and leave me here. I don't need you."

He frowned down at her, not hiding his displeasure, and waited for her to back down. Most people did. She looked him straight in the eye and stuck her chin out even farther. That beautiful, stubborn chin. Before Madison, he would have said he preferred a more agreeable woman. He couldn't remember the last time anyone had corrected him, never mind lectured him on his behavior. He found her direct challenge more exciting than any striptease or act of seduction. He wanted to kiss that stubbornness right out of her—slowly, all night, if that's what it took. As his blood rushed downward, he found himself softening his stance and admitting, "I thought you were gone for good."

Madison looked down, then back up at him, this time through her long lashes. "And that wasn't a cause for celebration?"

His hands tightened on the front of the coat he'd wrapped around her, and he pulled her ever so slightly closer. "Surprisingly, no." He studied her delicate features and surprised himself by saying, "You could have been hurt."

"I'm fine," she said huskily, staring up at him as she had the night before. Tempting him.

He gave in to the temptation and kissed her parted lips. She met his kiss eagerly. He'd been half hoping that he'd built their attraction up in his mind. She wasn't his type. He didn't like complications, and she was definitely complicated.

And distracting. Here he was, kissing her on the side of the road instead of working in his restaurant, as he should have been. The sparks that flew between them burned away his reservations. He wanted her with a desperation that made everything else irrelevant. He pulled her closer, enjoying the feel of her against him, and wishing they were somewhere more private so he could strip away the layers that separated them.

She opened her mouth for him, and he lost what was left of his coherence as his tongue met hers in an intimate and passionate dance. What she lacked in experience, she made up for in sweet enthusiasm.

A car drove by and honked, reminding Richard of their very public location. He pulled back, tracing her still-parted lips with his thumb, loving that she looked as dazed by their kiss as he felt. "Let's go back to my house," he said huskily. He'd told himself he would give her time. The last hour hadn't changed the fact that she was an innocent, and a troubled one at that. Doing anything but sending her packing was a mistake, but he couldn't help himself. He wanted her, and by the way her eyes darkened with desire, he knew the feeling was mutual.

She nodded wordlessly.

He opened the passenger door, helped her in, and—unable to stop himself—stole one final kiss when she looked up after buckling herself in. He reluctantly broke off their connection and rushed around to the driver's seat. He almost backed into the stone wall across the street in his haste to turn his vehicle around.

He was going to take Maddy to his bed, and, although it was something he never did, he was going to skip work to stay with her in the morning. Some experiences were not meant to be rushed.

He took her hand in his during the short drive back to his house, kissing the back of it, then turning it over to taste the inside of her wrist. It was both a torture and a delight to have access to so little of her. He met her eyes for a potent moment and, in as close to an apology as he could come, said, "I can drive you to a hotel if you'd like, but I want to be with you, Madison. You're all I've thought about today, to the point where I didn't care about anything else but coming back to you and tasting your sweet kiss again. I want to take you to my bed and spend the whole night savoring you. Tell me now if this is not what you also want." He laid her hand high on his thigh.

Her hand moved, cupping him in an exploratory fashion, and she gave him a shy smile. "Didn't you say you don't sleep with virgins?"

A slow smile spread across his face.

"I changed my mind."

Me, too. I do not want to be rescued from this. Madison took out her phone and texted Gino, momentarily breaking off her connection with Richard. "Need one more day. Please don't come now."

Gino didn't respond, which was either a good sign or a very bad one. There was a slim chance—like, win-the-lottery slim—that he hadn't noticed she'd turned her phone on. If that was the case, turning it off was a good idea.

Of course, if she turned her phone off, she wouldn't know if he was on his way. And since there wasn't a locked door that could keep a man like Gino out, his barging in had the potential to bring her night with Richard to an abrupt halt.

I'm not experienced enough to know for sure, but I'm going to guess that a bodyguard breaking down his front door is not one of Richard's erotic fantasies.

"Who are you texting?" Richard asked.

"My—um—cousin?" *At least, that's what my father calls him. Oh, this is going to kill the mood, I just know it.* "He may be on his way to pick me up. I turned my phone on when I got lost. Gino may use the signal to find me."

Richard pulled the car into the driveway and turned in his seat to face her. "Why would he come simply because your phone is on?"

"He's always used my phone signal to track me. I never minded before. It saved me from having to always tell him where I was going," Maddy said, then realized how odd that might sound without further explanation. "He's also my bodyguard."

"Who are you?"

I'm going to die a virgin. "Madison Andrade."

"Andrade? As in Andrade Global?"

It wasn't a surprise that he knew the company—Stephan's company was always in the news. "That's my cousin's company. Alessandro Andrade is my father. He built

Andrade Technologies."

He looked her over again and whistled in a less-than-complimentary way. "You're the daughter of one of the wealthiest men in America?"

Worse than measles, I carry the dreaded wealth germ.

"You're not scared and running from a bad situation. You're Daddy's little pissed off princess trying to teach him a lesson."

She replied defensively, "That's not true."

"Really? This isn't about getting back at your family by breaking their rules?"

"No." *Shit, what if he's right? What if that's all this is?* "It isn't like that," she denied hotly, but even as she said it she wasn't sure. "I—" She stopped there.

"Yes?"

Nothing. Nothing that makes sense. She closed her eyes for a painful moment and said, "Why can't you be nice?"

"What's the matter, Princess, not used to people being honest with you?"

"Don't call me that."

Leaning back against the driver's door, he raised an eyebrow and asked, "Who do you live with?"

Between gritted teeth, Maddy admitted, "My parents."

"Do you have a job?"

"No."

"BMW or Mercedes for graduation?"

"A 1980 Boeing 747 jet. I like vintage."

"Go home, Princess. I'm not interested."

"Then stop kissing me," she said angrily. "I'm getting

pretty tired of you judging me. You don't know me. And you don't have to. Gino is probably on his way. You can go back to eating your way around France for all I care."

He sat back and sighed. "Did that analogy sound as ridiculous when I used it last night?"

Maddy crossed her arms over her chest and said, "Worse."

"I'm sorry." Those dark eyes seared through her.

I did not see that coming. "It's okay, you were being honest."

He turned toward her. "No, I wasn't. I was trying to keep you out of my bed."

She lowered her arms, undid her seatbelt, turned to face him, and whispered, "Why?"

"Because of this." He threaded his hand through her hair and pulled her into a savage kiss. There was no teasing, no tempting, just a bold claiming of her mouth. His tongue plunged and withdrew, leaving her feeling shaken and yearning to be filled again. She opened her mouth wider for him in an invitation he accepted greedily.

When he broke the kiss off and rested his forehead on hers, their heavy breathing blended. Eyes still closed, Maddy said shakily, "I'm no expert, but what's wrong with it? It feels pretty damn good to me."

Taking her face in both hands, he kissed her open lips hungrily, then said, "Too good. Being with you, taking you to my bed and tasting every inch of you, is all I can think about."

Maddy opened her eyes and met his. "And that's a problem because you'll eventually want to eat at other restaurants?"

He shook his head and frowned with impatience. "Forget that stupid analogy."

"I can't promise that. I'm only human." She shot him a cheeky smile.

"You drive me crazy, do you know that?" he growled and nipped softly at her neck. "I've been telling myself all day that if you weren't at my house when I returned it would be for the best. Now that I know who you are, I'm even more convinced that you don't belong here."

"Because my family has money?"

"Because I had to fight for everything I have. I have no respect for those who take the easy road."

Maddy pulled away from him and sat back. "What happened to make you so defensive? First you're upset because you think I'm after money, now you're upset because I have it. I don't have a problem with money. You do."

He closed his eyes for a moment. "You're right."

Maddy sat up straight in surprise. "Really? Which part? I mean, of course I am."

In the silence that followed, the air was charged with the sizzle of their attraction, but also with a connection that defied explanation. It didn't matter if it made sense or not. It simply was.

"Money ruins more lives than it saves. I'm not interested in having more than I need to pay the bills. Until you, I didn't realize how strongly I felt on the subject."

In his eyes, she saw how an old pain still tormented him. "Why?"

He looked out the car window as if he were looking back in time. "My mother put money before the welfare of her children. Alyson and I were accessories she packed and moved into the mansion of each new husband she had. One fake family after the next. I learned not to care, not to get attached. I wanted a family, but what I got instead was a new car every year. I'm afraid her lifestyle left me with a disgust for the wealthy."

Maddy thought of her family and knew, despite their present issues, that that wasn't the life they'd given her. "She may have been trying to provide for her children the only way she knew how."

His face twisted with disdain. "No, we were not her priority. Her third husband tried to force himself on Alyson when she was seventeen. She ran away to escape him. My mother took her husband's side. I believe she wanted to wait out the time limit built into the prenuptial."

With a gasp, Maddy covered her mouth and asked, "What did you do?"

Looking past her as he remembered, he said, "I nearly killed him when I found out. Then I followed Alyson. She'd come here, to Sablet, looking for our real father."

"Did you find him?"

"No, but we found his old house. They say he died here, practically penniless after my mother left him. In a house that was mortgaged to the hilt. The locals say during their marriage he took out loans in an attempt to appease her, but it wasn't enough. She needed more."

"That's so sad. And then you bought the house?"

"In the beginning, Alyson wanted to live here. Eventually, she made friends in town and moved out."

"But you stayed."

"Sablet was as good a place as any to open a restaurant."

She put her hand on his clenched one. "I think it was more than that."

He shrugged like he was dismissing her claim, but then he admitted, "I barely remember my father. I was five years old when we left. There is something here I haven't been able to let go of."

Family. The only one he'd ever known. Maddy's heart broke a bit for him. She didn't know what to say, so she leaned across the divide and kissed him with an urgency that surprised both of them. She wanted to kiss away his pain, kiss away her doubts and whatever else stood between them.

He pulled her to him in a crushing embrace, pulling her shirt free of her slacks so his rough hands could slide beneath and span her small back. Between kisses he said, "I'll never be a wealthy man."

She pulled his shirt free and began to unbutton it. "I don't care."

He groaned and kissed her deeply, running a hand beneath her shirt to cup one of her breasts possessively. "I hope you mean that, because I've never wanted anyone as much as I want you. Once you're mine, I may have to keep you."

Feeling giddy with passion, Maddy jokingly warned, "Sample my cooking and there's no more eating out."

His chest rumbled with laughter even as he unclipped her bra with one hand and gave her bared nipple a light pinch with his other. It hardened beneath his touch, and heat spread through Maddy all the way to the tips of her curling toes. "I want more than a sample, Madison. I want it all. Tell me you want it, too."

She breathed her answer against his lips: "I do."

"Let's go inside," he growled and kissed her one last time before sprinting around the car to open her door. She'd barely had time to step out of the car before he swung her up in his arms.

After a briefly pausing to open the door, he sprinted down the hall and up the stairs to his bedroom. He slowed only to lay her across his bed. She was breathing as heavily as he was when their eyes met and held.

"Are you sure?" he asked, his eyes burning with need for her.

She swallowed hard and nodded.

He sat beside her on the bed. "Have you ever had an orgasm?"

She blushed and shook her head.

"Not even one you gave yourself?"

Her cheeks warmed more and she looked away.

He pulled her to her feet and undressed her slowly. When she was standing naked and exposed before him, he slid his hand down her stomach and cupped her sex. "You will come again and again until you are begging to feel me inside you. A woman's first time is one she remembers her whole life. It should be one worth remembering, *non?*"

Oh, God, yes. Maddy nodded and licked her lips.

"Turn around," he ordered.

She did.

"Kneel on the bed."

When she hesitated, he put his hand on her back and guided her forward to the edge of the bed, whispering hotly in her ear from behind: "Trust me."

She crawled on the bed and waited, facing away from him, as excited as she was nervous. He applied pressure to her back again until she was bent before him on all fours. He whispered to her to lower herself down onto her elbows. She would have twisted herself like a pretzel had he asked in that seductive French accent. He sunk to his knees behind her. His hands came around the front of her thighs and spread them. Then he opened her lower lips. His tongue plunged inside her. She gasped and instinctively tried to pull away in surprise, but he held her in place. He stilled and she relaxed.

Gripping the sheets in front of her, she bit her lip when his tongue repeated its exploration. He lapped her exposed clit and blew on it, then drove his tongue inside her again. She shuddered and pushed back eagerly against his mouth.

With the same talent with which he'd claimed her mouth earlier, he teased and pleasured her inside and out with his tongue until she was crying from the intensity of it. Only then did he thrust a finger into her soaked opening and pump while he suckled her clit.

Heat spread and exploded within her, and she cried out with the intensity of her first orgasm. She was still shaking from it when he withdrew his finger and ordered, "That's only the beginning. Roll onto your back for me."

She did and he pulled her forward until her feet were

almost touching the floor beside his knees. His hands cupped her breasts, circling her, lightly pinching her nipples until they were both throbbing painfully and begging for the hot, wet attention of his mouth. He pushed her back, holding her in place with one firm hand on her stomach and blew on her dripping sex until she parted her legs wider and whimpered.

He nipped her quivering thigh. "You taste so damn good," he growled and sank his tongue back into her, this time grazing a spot that sent her nearly into a convulsion of pleasure. His hands slid beneath her buttocks and raised her to give himself better access. Once again his tongue delved and lapped. His teeth teased her excited nub until she gripped his head and held him to her as she neared her second orgasm. He rolled her clit between his thumb and finger then started to rub it with a speed that had her throwing back her head and begging him not to stop.

Thankfully he didn't, at least not until she came for the second time in her life.

As her breathing returned to normal, she asked shakily, "At which point do *you* get naked?" She peered up at him. He was still fully dressed between her bare legs.

His smile was the sexiest thing she'd ever seen. "When you tell me to."

Two could play this game. She smiled impishly up at him. "And if I never do?"

"I find enough pleasure watching you come that I could from just touching you." He stood, took both of her hands in his, and hauled her to her feet. Without saying a word, he put her hands behind her back and held them with one of his. The action arched her breasts, something he immediately took advantage of. He kissed one, then the other. His hot breath warmed her skin and sent shivers of pleasure through her. Then his teeth closed gently on one of her nipples and tugged softly. He said, "Some women can come just from this. Let's see if you're one of those women." He suckled her, lapped her, sent her into a shuddering mess while his free hand claimed one of her buttocks possessively.

She writhed against his mouth and whimpered with need. The brush of his clothed legs against her bare legs reminded her he was in control. It was time to change that. Held immobile before him, she used what she had to excite him—her words. "I want you, Richard. Inside me. Please take me, Richard. Now."

He didn't need to be told twice.

He stepped back and shed his clothing. His hand shook a bit as he sheathed himself in a condom. Kissing wildly, they fell back on the bed together and he braced himself above her. Their eyes met and held as he positioned himself between her legs. "I'll be gentle," he promised.

She opened herself wider for him and gasped as his tip entered her.

"You're so tight," he groaned.

She wrapped her arms around his neck and kissed him deeply. He slowly entered her with gentle thrusts, each time going a bit deeper. Twinges of discomfort were quickly replaced by the wonder of how good he felt inside her. He took his time, letting her adjust to his size. Then he began to move inside her with a rhythm as old as time. It was better, so much better than she'd ever imagined. He kissed her neck, whispering things in French to her that, although she couldn't understand, sent her into a hot frenzy.

His hands were everywhere, exploring, and guiding hers. She felt a warmth spread through her stomach and began to sob from the pleasure. His pace increased until he was pounding into her and she was wildly crying out his name.

Spent, he collapsed onto her, bracing himself above her so his weight didn't crush her. He buried his face in her neck, and she gloried in the feel of him still inside her and the loud beat of his heart. A beat that grew louder and louder until she realized that it wasn't his heartbeat at all, but someone knocking on the downstairs main door. Banging, actually—angrily and with increasing force.

Richard raised his head as he, too, heard it. He rolled off her and swore in French. In all his naked glory he walked to the window and cursed again. "Does your cousin drive a limousine?"

Wrapping a sheet hastily around her, Maddy went to the window and stood beside him. She doubted anyone below could see them, but there was a chance. She gasped when she saw two couples outlined in the dim light of the driveway. "Oh, my God, Gino brought my parents. And Aunt Katrine and Uncle Vic, too."

Misunderstanding the distress in her voice, Richard pulled her into his arms and said, "I won't let them hurt you."

Looking from Richard back to her family and then back to Richard, Maddy groaned nervously. “It’s not me I’m worried about.”

Chapter Five

MADDY SCRAMBLED INTO her clothing. Richard rushed to dress, not because he was intimidated by whoever was testing the strength of his front door, but because he didn't want Maddy to face them alone. They flew down the stairs side by side.

In the main hall of his house, Madison stopped and looked up at him with a concern he wished he had time to kiss away. She took him by the hand and said, "It's probably better if I go out there alone."

He wasn't used to anyone worrying about him. He kissed her lightly on the lips. "I can take care of myself."

Her eyes rounded with real worry. "My father can be—intimidating."

He didn't like the way that sounded. "Are you afraid of him?"

She shook her head adamantly. "No. Of course not. But if he thinks he needs to protect me, he won't be kind to you. He has old-world views on family. This could get ugly."

Tucking a loose curl behind Madison's ear, Richard assured her, "It'll be fine."

Drawing in a fortifying breath, Madison nodded and opened the door.

Gino practically fell forward into the hall. Ranting in Italian, he swung her up into a bone-crushing hug. When he put her down, he chastised her as one would a child. "You stole ten years off my life, Maddy, when you did not call me. Never do that again."

It was not the exchange Richard had expected to see. His surprise increased when Madison's response to his angry tone was to wrap her arms around the giant's waist and hug him back. "I'm so sorry, Gino. It was a spontaneous decision and one that I now wish I had handled differently."

Real love shone in the older man's eyes as he smoothed her hair. "You're safe. That's what matters. But next time you have a crazy idea, let me in on it. I'd rather face your father's wrath than worry that you've been taken."

"Is he angry with me?" Madison asked.

"Livid," Gino answered. Nodding at Richard, he continued, "He should stay inside."

Madison looked over her shoulder at Richard, wordlessly offering him the option one last time. Richard stepped forward and offered his hand to Gino in greeting. "Richard D'Argenson. I am looking forward to meeting Madison's parents."

Gino looked back and forth between them, then shook Richard's hand. "You're one brave bastard."

"Not really, but I would never send her out there alone."

Releasing Richard's hand, Gino nodded in approval. "That might save you." He turned and led the way out onto the steps.

A short, brown-haired woman came rushing forward and tearfully threw her arms around Madison. She searched the younger woman's face and said, "I was so worried. When we received your text and Gino admitted he didn't know where you were, I imagined all sorts of scenarios."

"Mom, I told you I was okay."

"Anyone could have sent that message to stall us from coming to find you. I've never been so scared in my life."

And I've never been so sorry. Tears began to run down Maddy's cheeks. "I didn't consider how awful it would be for you. I needed time away from everyone to think." Her mother kept hugging her, tighter and tighter, until Maddy said, "Mom, are you okay?"

With a prolonged, pained laugh, her mother released her. "I want to kill you, but I love you so I can't. I'm hugging you, but I'd like to strangle you a little. I mean that in the most loving, you'd-better-never-do-anything-like-this-again way." Then she started crying.

A tall, expensively dressed Italian man in his early sixties stepped toward the emotional pair. His voice boomed. "Thinking is all you'd better have been doing here." His disgust for Richard rang clear in his tone.

Madison stepped away from her mother and moved to stand next to Richard. She took his hand in hers and faced her father defiantly. "You told me to grow up, Dad, and that's what I did."

With a snarl, her father reached for Richard. "I'll kill him."

Another man, about his age and stature, stepped forward

and said, "I haven't punched anyone in thirty years, but I have your back if you need me, Alessandro."

Richard assessed the two older men. In their prime they might have been deadly, but age had softened them a bit. As long as the fight didn't include the bodyguard, he was pretty confident he'd win. Still, this was Madison's family. Diffusing the situation would be better for all involved. "I don't blame you for wanting to hit me, sir. If the situation were reversed, I might want to do the same thing, but . . ."

"But nothing," Alessandro roared. "How dare you take advantage of my daughter and then have the nerve to think I'd do anything but ruin you?"

Richard's temper began to rise along with his accuser's. "I am only being civil for Madison's sake. On any other occasion I would have already thrown your elderly ass off my property."

Alessandro growled something in Italian and stepped toward him.

Richard growled back in French, dropped Madison's hand, and met him halfway.

Victor interjected, "As long as he doesn't run, I'm in." When Alessandro paused to look at his brother, Victor shrugged. "I'm only ten months out of my knee replacement surgery. They said no running."

Madison stepped between Richard and her father and put a hand on both their chests. Her cheeks were red with anger. "If you touch Richard, Dad, I will never forgive you." To Richard's surprise, she then turned her displeasure toward him. "And you, watch your temper. He's in his sixties, for God's sake. A fight could give him a heart attack."

The remaining visitor, a tall blonde woman who had been quiet up to that point, started clapping. "You tell 'em, Maddy." When her husband frowned at her, the woman Madison had referred to as Aunt Katrine smiled sweetly at him. "I'm not saying I condone how she ran off, but look what she ran to." She winked at Richard. "I wouldn't let you mess up that face, either. Let the poor girl enjoy her first boyfriend."

Madison's mother laid a hand on her husband's arm and addressed Richard. "Instead of continuing this brawl in your driveway, why don't you invite us inside . . ." She paused when she came to what she didn't yet know.

After releasing a long breath, Richard supplied his name. "Richard D'Argenson." Then he added, "You are all more than welcome to come inside. It's a cold night."

No one moved at first. Richard sensed if he softened his stance now Madison's father would never respect him, and for some reason that was becoming important to him.

"Thank you, Richard. I'm Elise, and the man who is glaring at you is my husband, Alessandro." She waved a hand at the other older Italian man. "This is Alessandro's brother, Victor, and his wife, Katrine. I believe you met our cousin, Gino."

In a somewhat absurdly polite exchange, considering the situation, Richard nodded to each and said, "It's a pleasure to meet you. Please, come inside for coffee."

"There is no way in hell I'm going to pretend—" Alessandro started, until his wife whispered something in his ear.

Then, although he didn't look happy about it, he resumed in a civil tone, even if it sounded a bit forced: "By all means, let's have coffee then."

Madison's worried eyes searched Richard's. She mouthed a silent, "I'm sorry."

He took her hand and raised it to his lips, even though the action gained him an audible hiss from her protective father. He pulled her close to him and, murmuring softly so no one else could hear, said, "I like them already."

✧ ✧ ✧

ONCE INSIDE, ELISE and Katrine flanked Richard. Under the guise of wanting to help him make coffee, they pried him away from Maddy and swept him into the kitchen with them.

Alone with her father and uncle, Maddy crossed her arms over her chest and prepared for a lecture. Her father closed the distance and, despite her rigid pose, pulled her into his arms. "I haven't slept since you disappeared. Why would you put us through this?"

Even as she fought back tears, she kept her arms folded between them. "I didn't mean to worry any of you." He held her back from him, and she found she was unable to lie to his face. "Okay, I did mean to. I was angry with you, and I wanted you to see how much what you'd told me hurt me."

She looked across at her uncle. "You, too, Uncle Vic. How could you lie to Stephan? How could you not tell him the truth now?"

Her uncle addressed her father: "I can't believe you told her."

Alessandro looked down into his daughter's eyes and said, "She asked me, and I've never lied to her."

Maddy shook her head angrily and pulled away. "I used to believe that was true, but I'm not sure anymore."

Her uncle defended his brother. "Alessandro never agreed with my decision, but he stands by my right to raise my children the way I think is correct."

Maddy snorted. "Stephan wasn't a child. He was my age."

"And he's successful now because he left his foolish California lifestyle behind him. I know you think he loved Nicole, but he was trying to get with her like she was some common tramp . . ." Victor's tirade tapered off as if he remembered why they were in Richard's house. "I'm not judging whatever happened here."

Angry for both herself and her cousin, Maddy said, "Yes, I slept with Richard, but that doesn't make me anything but a normal woman in her twenties, and I'm not going to apologize for that. This is not the old world. I love you, Uncle Vic, but your values are not mine. And they weren't Stephan's. I don't want to be there the day he finds out what you've done. So, if you're feeling self-righteous, take a closer look at yourself. I'm not ashamed of my decisions, but I am of yours."

An angry red spread across her uncle's face. "Alessandro, you're going to let your daughter talk to me that way?"

Maddy's father rubbed his hands over his face roughly,

then said, "Maddy has a right to voice her opinion."

Victor turned angrily on his brother. "Do you agree with her?"

With a pained shrug, Alessandro said, "I don't know. I've never lied to Maddy, and"—his face tightened a bit and a muscle in his jaw twitched—"even when she knows I don't want to hear it, she has never lied to me. I may not like the truth, but I would rather know it."

"I did what I thought was right."

Alessandro went over to his brother and put a hand of support on his shoulder. "I know you did. And I've done a lot of thinking over the last few days. If Maddy needs to tell Stephan the truth, then that's what she has to do. No matter what the consequences are. She must also do what she thinks is right."

Watching her uncle shrink a bit before her father brought new tears to Maddy's eyes. Victor said, "I hope to God we don't lose him over this."

Maddy reached out and took her uncle's hand in hers. "I don't want to cause trouble, Uncle Vic. I don't want to hurt anyone. If you promise me you'll tell him, I'll honor your secret."

Her uncle's eyes misted over and he nodded. "You're a good girl, Maddy."

Her eyebrows shot up in challenge. "Even if I'm a tramp?"

He blushed at her jab.

Alessandro interjected, "About that. You're not staying here."

"Dad, I'm old enough to know what I'm doing."

"Apparently not, or you wouldn't have run away in the first place."

Ouch.

"And you're lucky your mother was here or your boyfriend wouldn't be looking so pretty. He was smart to hide in the kitchen with the women."

"He's not hiding. He spends his life in a kitchen. He's a chef."

"A chef?" both men asked in unison in similar tones of disdain.

Putting her hands on her hips, Maddy said in a huff, "It's a perfectly respectable profession, and I won't have you looking down on him."

As if she weren't in the room anymore, her uncle said, "You should tell her *to* stay here. She's always been a bit contrary."

"Oh, she's coming home with us," her father said.

Shaking her head, Maddy said, "Where's Mom? I can't talk to you about this."

✧ ✧ ✧

RICHARD WAS SHOWING Elise and Katrine how to make a traditional holiday dessert when he stopped and smiled. They were both paying close attention and shared not only his passion for good food but also a keen appreciation for the process.

After he had briefly described his restaurant to them,

Elise had said something that had touched his heart. "My grandmother always said that the reason a family recipe is impossible for others to duplicate is because the most important ingredient is love. You can't go wrong if that's where you start."

He'd nodded in agreement but didn't admit the truth: He didn't have a family recipe. Not one. He'd created his own dishes, and that had always been enough until now. His father's house had once given him a sense of family, but after meeting Madison's family, it would never again feel like more than a cold stone structure.

This was family. They yelled. They worried. They protected each other. Maddy might have had a reason to leave them, but there was no doubt they loved her.

As I could.

The realization shook him. He'd heard couples say they knew from the moment they met that they were meant to be together. He'd always scoffed at the idea, until Madison. He had tried to push her away, tried to fight the attraction, but in the end he admitted to himself that the more time he spent with her, the less he wanted to imagine his life without her.

As if she'd heard his thoughts, she walked into the kitchen and crossed the room to stand by him. When she saw he was cooking with her mother, she smiled. "Did you survive the grilling?"

He swept her hair over her shoulder, kissed her neck gently, and said, "Easily. Your mother and aunt are incredible."

She jumped as her father and uncle entered the kitchen,

then asked, "And my father?"

Richard put a supportive arm around her waist. "He loves you. That much is obvious. You're lucky to have someone who cares enough to be angry with you."

Maddy smiled up at him. "Thank you for giving us time to talk. We've at least come to an understanding."

Fear seared through him. "Does that mean you're leaving with them?" Of course she was. Why wouldn't she? Because of one day they'd been together? Because of one romp in his bed? She'd run away to prove a point to her parents, and sleeping with him had driven that point home.

"Do you want me to?" she asked softly.

His heart clenched in his chest. "No," he admitted huskily.

Madison straightened her shoulders with resolve and looked at her father. "Then let's feed him and see if it softens his mood."

Although he had no doubt that her family had house staff, none of them seemed the least bit bothered when he said he didn't and requested that they each carry something into the dining room. Her father and uncle took plates and saucers from their wives and dutifully followed Richard. Elise handed Gino the coffee pot and he ferried it into the next room as if he'd done it a hundred times before.

When they were settled around the table, Richard said, "Had I known you would be here for Christmas Eve I would have planned *le Réveillon* feast. Instead, I hope you will accept *la bûche de Noël.* It is a chocolate and chestnut cake rolled like a log and filled with cream. Normally, I would adorn it with a bit more, but time did not allow this, you understand."

Alessandro leaned toward his wife and said, "I can't look at him and eat."

"Dad, we can hear you," Maddy said with a sigh.

"Let it go, Madison, it's okay," Richard reassured. He took her hand in full view of everyone. "He won't like me until he knows me, and I'm not going anywhere."

Elise touched her husband's arm and said, "It's been a stressful day for all of us. Alessandro's tired. We're all tired. But thank you for welcoming us, Richard." She rested her head on her husband's shoulder and said, "Do you realize that this is the first Christmas Eve that I'm not cooking?"

Alessandro kissed his wife's forehead and said, "You sound sad about that."

"I'll miss your mother's meatballs. And the chocolate tortellis your grandmother taught me to make. I'm happy we found Maddy, but it's strange to not be with the rest of the family."

Some of Alessandro's earlier softening disappeared when he looked across the table at his daughter. "This is the first Christmas since Maddy was born that we aren't all together."

Victor interjected, "We can rectify that if we leave soon. I don't sleep well on planes, but at least we'll be home."

Raising her chin, Maddy announced, "I won't be going with you."

Feeling her hand go cold beneath his, Richard knew what her declaration had cost her, and he said, "You can, Madison. I'm not going anywhere, except to follow you if you don't eventually return."

She met his eyes and what he saw there hit him like a punch to the gut. "I'm not leaving you, Richard."

Standing up, Alessandro threw his napkin on his empty plate and said, "Enough. I have been more than understanding. I am sick to here"—he raised a hand to the top of his head—"with understanding. No more. Maddy, we are going home now, and you are coming with us."

Madison stood, her chin set proudly and at the same angle as her father's stubborn one. Richard wondered if Alessandro knew how alike he and his daughter were. "No, I am not. I want to stay in France. Maybe study French at the university. I'm not leaving Sablet until I'm ready to."

She's not leaving. His heart thudded joyfully in his chest. He gave her hand a reassuring squeeze. She looked down at him and he nodded. *Yes. Stay with me.*

"Don't push me, Maddy. You are . . ." her father boomed.

Elise stood beside her husband and lightly touched his shoulder. "Alessandro, sit down. Sit down before you lose your daughter."

He glared at his wife. "She's coming home with us."

Elise looked at her daughter, then up at her husband, and shook her head. "If you push her, she'll choose him."

"She doesn't even know him," Alessandro stormed.

Taking one of his hands in hers, Elise chided, "How long did it take you to decide that you wanted to marry me?"

His expression softened with the memory. "I knew the first time you said my name."

With tears in her eyes, Elise smiled up at him. "It was the same for me. And we were younger. What would we have done if my father had tried to separate us?"

He shook his head in resignation. "Anything and everything it took to stay together. And he would have failed." Alessandro pulled his wife to his chest and rested his chin on the top of her head. He closed his eyes and said, "What is a man to do when his daughter is as stubborn as her mother?"

"Me?" Elise squealed. "You think she takes after *me*?"

A deep laugh rumbled out of Alessandro and the tension of the moment dissolved. In that exchange, Richard had seen more love and loyalty than he'd witnessed in his life, and it inspired him to take a leap of faith and trust what he felt for Maddy. He gently pulled her down to sit beside him. Her father and mother returned to their seats.

The short silence that followed was broken by Victor's exclaiming, "Oh, my God, this has to be the best chocolate cake I have ever tasted."

Katrine laughed and chastised him, "Victor, how can you eat a time like this?"

Victor shrugged and dug into the cake with his fork again. "I thought we might be going and it seemed a shame not to at least taste it." He offered the next bite to her. "Try it."

The tall blonde shook her head. "You know I have to watch my diet. It's too easy to put on weight at our age."

Wiggling his eyebrows at his wife, Victor said, "We could burn it off later at the hotel."

Maddy buried her face in Richard's chest and said, "You

can still back out if you want to. This is my life."

Richard eased her back a bit so he could look into her eyes. "I wouldn't change a thing about you or them. Did you mean what you said about staying and studying here?"

"Yes."

He kissed her lightly on the lips, then looked at her parents. "I don't want to be the reason your family is apart this year. There are several unused bedrooms in this house and enough hotels nearby if needed. It would be an honor if your family celebrated Christmas in my home. I'll cook."

Elise hopped with excitement beside her husband. "Christmas in Provence. Let's do it, Alessandro." He didn't stand a chance against his wife's plea. She looked down at her watch. "It's almost seven. We have time to charter something big enough to bring them all over."

Maddy asked, "Do you think Stephan will come?"

Katrine looked sadly at her husband and said, "He works so much right now, it's hard to say. All he thinks about is competing with Dominic Corisi. I worry about him."

Maddy appeared to want to say more on the subject. She and her uncle exchanged a meaningful look, but she kept her thoughts to herself.

Alessandro announced, "I'll bring the family here, but that doesn't mean I'm okay with Maddy living with a man no one knows."

Madison stood and walked around the table to her father. "I can find a place in town. I would like to take French language classes. I know you're not happy with my decision, but I do want to stay here."

Alessandro stood and hugged his daughter. Then he cleared his throat and said, "Find two apartments, because Gino will need a place to stay, too." When Maddy would have said something, Alessandro addressed Richard instead. "It looks like the Andrades are having a *Joyeux Noël* this year. Are you sure you're ready to meet the whole family?"

How many could there be? Richard shrugged. "Certainly."

Maddy put her hands on her hips and said, "Dad, you can't invite them all."

Looking far too pleased with himself, Alessandro sat back in his chair and cut himself a slice of chocolate cake. "You heard your boyfriend. He wants to meet them."

Maddy returned to sit beside Richard. "I hope you like chaos, Richard, because that is what will be flying over—multiple generations of it."

Richard looked around the table and said, "I have had a—how do you say—an epiphany this week. In my work, I require order and control. In my home life, I am beginning to see the benefits of a little crazy."

Quick smiles faded as everyone pondered if his revelation was an insult or a compliment, then returned as they got his dry sense of humor.

He gave them his most handsome, toothy grin.

Different as they were from him, Richard had found what he'd yearned for when he'd purchased his father's house—a place to belong. With Maddy and, with any luck, her family.

"How many should I prepare for?" Richard asked.

"At least thirty," Maddy said.

Thirty. Holy Hell. "I should start cooking soon then."

Katrine offered, "Would you like us to stay and help?"

"Only if you will teach me how to make a good Italian sauce."

Elise raised her hands and face heavenward and said, "You hear that, Nonna?" She paused as if receiving an answer. "I know. I like him, too."

Chapter Six

SOMETIME ON CHRISTMAS night, Richard and Maddy snuck out the back door of his house. The laughter and boisterous voices that filtered outside became fainter the deeper they walked into the garden. They stopped at a stone bench and sat side by side.

Maddy said, "You did it. You survived an Andrade Christmas."

"Your family is not as bad as you think."

"You can say that even after they dressed you up as Santa and had all the young cousins sit on your lap and pull your beard?"

Richard laughed and hugged Maddy to his side. "Your father is still testing me and that's okay. He wants only the best for you."

"What does your sister think of my family?"

"She's still here, isn't she? Usually she stays for an hour and goes back to her friends in town. Maybe because your male cousins are flocking around her?"

"Tell her to watch out for those Italian men. They're trouble, just like the French." Maddy laid her head on

Richard's shoulder. "Hey, I thought you should know I apologized to her for not being honest about why I was on the run. I felt like an idiot, but she took it well."

"She doesn't hold grudges, not even when she should." Maddy knew instantly who he was referencing.

"Did you call your mother? It's Christmas."

"Birthing a child does not make a woman a mother," Richard said coldly.

"You should call her."

"Not everyone has the family you have. I won't push you to tell me what made you run, but I have to say I can't understand it. I want to understand, though."

Maddy slid a hand beneath Richard's jacket and laid it on his heart. "I am not a good secret keeper, Richard. Sometimes I get so wrapped up in trying to help people that I share things I shouldn't. But this is different. I discovered something that could unravel the very fabric of my family. You want to know why I ran? Because I didn't want to keep a secret I didn't agree with and I couldn't live with being the one to expose it. I can't tell you what it is. Honestly, I want to forget that I know it."

"So, what will you do?"

"I'll find an apartment in Sablet and study French." She looked at him from beneath her lashes and added, "And if you'd like, we could see each other often."

"I like," Richard growled and claimed her mouth with a passionate kiss. He continued to whisper in her ear in French. Maddy couldn't understand much of what he said, but the way his hands possessively ran over her made translation unnecessary.

"Maddy," her father's voice called from the door into the darkness, "are you out there?"

Maddy broke off the kiss and buried her face in Richard's chest. "Don't answer."

Breathing as raggedly as she was, Richard hugged her close and chuckled. "If we say nothing, he'll likely send Gino out to find us."

Maddy arched upward and murmured against Richard's lips, "Just a few more minutes."

"You challenge my good sense, Maddy. But I can't say no to you," Richard answered and kissed her deeply again.

✧ ✧ ✧

A FEW DAYS later, Richard pulled into his driveway after leaving his restaurant and noticed a light on in one of the windows. His sister had a key and there was no evidence of a forced entry, so he called out in French as he entered, "Hello? Who is here?"

His eyes caught a movement, and he dropped the plate of food he'd brought home as he realized who it was. There, halfway up the stairs, stood a perfectly naked Maddy leaning seductively against the railing.

A huge smile spread across her face and she bent over laughing. "I am so happy that you're alone. I did not think about how embarrassing this would be if you brought a friend home for dinner."

She walked down the steps as she spoke and Richard

could not find the faculties to speak. They hadn't been alone since their first night together. He finally swallowed hard and asked, "Where's Gino?"

Maddy continued her slow-motion decent toward him. Those beautiful pert breasts bounced with each step. She wore her hair down, and one of her nipples played peekaboo from behind it each time she moved. She stopped barely a foot in front of him and smiled up at him, a combination of innocence and siren. "Circling the neighborhood. I convinced him the only way he would know where I was at all times was if he let me go where I wanted. And I want to be with you." She looked behind him with humor in her eyes. "But only if you close the door, because I'm fucking freezing."

He kicked the door closed behind him, put the food down, and pulled her into his arms. "Your family doesn't want you here with me." Even as he spoke he stopped caring that her parents had asked both of them to take it slowly.

Fast. Slow. It didn't matter. He wanted to take her again and again, here on the stairs, later in his bed. It had been days since the first time he'd been with her, and a need to have her again had been building inside him.

She laced her fingers behind his neck and said, "Let me worry about them. I don't want to sleep in bed by myself in town, wishing I were here in yours."

Richard kissed her deeply, then growled, "Who said we would make it to the bed?"

He lifted her and carried her to the bottom of the stairs. "Let's play a game, *ma puce*. There are twenty stairs leading to the bedroom. We'll stop on each one. You tell me what you want and I'll do it, whatever it is. Then we'll move up a stair and it'll be my turn to tell you what I want. Let's see if we make it to the top."

Maddy's eyes widened. "What if it's something I don't want to do."

His daring little American virgin. It was easy to forget that their last time had been her first. "Even when you're having sex with yourself you should care if your partner enjoys it."

Maddy's eyes rounded more. "Who is your partner when you're having sex with yourself?"

"It was a joke," Richard said with a chuckle. "A joke that was funny in my head but lost something in translation, I think."

"I think I get it." Maddy shot him a huge smile, and in that moment of uninhibited joy, Richard knew he would never see a more beautiful woman. She glanced over her shoulder at the steps behind her and asked, "Were you also joking about the stairs?"

"No," he said and kissed her sweet smile. "Think of it as having ten sex wishes."

Maddy's mouth fell open. She looked adorably worried. "I can think of about three things I'd like. Maybe four."

Richard kissed her again and said, "It's our game, Maddy. I'll help you if you run out of ideas. But you have to start. Tell me what you want."

She liked that. He could tell. She looked him over said, "You need to strip."

"Strip?" He cocked his head to the side. "Oh, you mean my clothes. Of course." He began to unbutton his shirt, then stopped. "Do you want me to take them off slowly or like I can't wait to fuck you?"

Maddy cleared her throat nervously. "Like the second one."

He tore off his shirt, stepped out of his shoes and socks, dropped his pants and threw them behind him onto the floor. Once freed, his cock stood high and fully erect between them. "Move up one step," he ordered.

Maddy did.

"Sit down. Spread your legs for me and rub yourself until you're wet."

Maddy didn't move at first. She looked away nervously, then back and said, "I thought this was about doing things to each other."

"For each other," he corrected. "You said you've never pleasured yourself. I want to see you learn to. I want to watch while you do it. Will you do that for me, Maddy? That's my first wish."

Maddy sat but self-consciously kept her knees together. "I don't think I could come with you watching."

Richard smiled and shrugged. "Maybe not the first time, but we won't know, will we, unless you try? You can say no, Maddy, and I'll pick again. But there is no shame in knowing your own body. And no need to be embarrassed in front of me. You are the most beautiful woman I've ever seen and you will become even more beautiful as you become comfortable with your own body. Sexy is on the outside, yes? But the more important sex happens up here." Richard pointed to his head. "When a woman puts aside her fears for her lover, there is nothing sexier."

Maddy hesitantly spread her legs and brought her hand to her own sex. She started to rub slowly, almost cautiously, all the while watching Richard's face. Richard took his cock into his own hand and pumped it slowly. Maddy rubbed a little faster and a rosy blush spread up her chest and neck. In the quiet of the house, the only sound was their breathing.

After a few minutes, Maddy's fingers were wet with her own juices and her eyes were heavy with desire. Richard asked himself what his last electricity bill had been in an attempt to slow himself down. He could have lost his load on her right there on the second step, but he didn't want to rush.

"Move up another step, Maddy."

Maddy lifted herself up one more step, leaving her legs wide and her dripping slit open to him. "I want you to lick me like you did that first night. I want to come in your mouth."

Richard sank down to his knees in between her legs. "My Maddy, I was hoping you'd say that." He parted her lower lips and blew gently on her clit before moving his chin back and forth over it. He watched her eyes as he tested what drove her the wildest. His teeth, his tongue, nipping, suckling, thrusting inside her. He took his time learning how best to please her, then maintained a rhythm he knew she enjoyed. She buried both of her hands in his hair and held him to her. He gripped her ass and lifted her so he could plunge his tongue deeper.

She was sweetness and boldness, and the taste of her drove him out of his mind with desire. He thrust his tongue in and out and alternated that with rubbing his chin back and forth over her clit. She cried out and he lapped her juices as they came.

He placed her back on the step and wiped his face with his hand. "Move up another step, Maddy." This time he stood and held onto the railing with one hand. "It's my turn, Maddy. Take me in your mouth. Bring me to where I just took you."

She took his cock in her hand, then almost shyly licked the side of it. She ran the tip of her tongue around the head of his cock and he shuddered. Her hot breath surrounded him, promising more. When she opened her mouth he had to restrain himself from jutting forward.

At first she took only an inch or so of him into her mouth. Richard groaned, wanting so much more. She opened her mouth wider, took him deeper, and Richard closed his eyes from the intensity of it. Her soft lips moved back and forth over the length of him while her tongue caressed him. She bobbed her head up and down on him. He gripped the hair on the back of her head and guided her to a rhythm that would bring him to climax. He watched her expression as he came deep in her mouth, loving how excited she looked as she drank his own juices.

She pulled her head back and her eyes were as feverish with desire as they had been when he'd been licking her. "Move up another step, Maddy."

She did so eagerly and Richard smiled. "Do you like this game, Maddy?"

She spread her legs and rubbed herself without his prompting. "I do. I really do."

"Slow down," Richard joked, even though he was pleased with how comfortable she was becoming with him. "We have sixteen more stairs and all night to get to the top."

✧ ✧ ✧

WINTER GAVE WAY to spring, spring blossomed into summer, and Richard fell slowly, hopelessly in love with Maddy. They spent every day together. In the beginning, being followed around by Gino had felt awkward, and Richard had resented it as much as Maddy did. Over time, though, he'd come to understand the commodity of immense wealth her family had made her. Gino was a constant reminder of what Maddy had walked away from to be with Richard.

If Maddy missed anything about her life in the United States, she never hinted at it. She enthusiastically signed up for French courses at a local school and had quickly made friends in the area. Richard had offered to teach her French himself, but she said when he spoke his native language she couldn't concentrate because it made her want to rip off her clothes and pounce him. Richard always smiled when he remembered the results of the first time he'd tested that theory. They'd been driving on a country road on their way to the coast. They never did make it to the beach. They'd made love in the car and ended up spontaneously renting a room at an inn they drove by. He'd spoken to Maddy in French often after that.

Sex with Maddy was incredible, but Richard was equally addicted to her presence in all other areas of his life. She opened the restaurant with him each morning, greeting his staff with such a big smile that they, too, fell in love with her, regardless of how she butchered their language. Bertrand flirted shamelessly with her, but Richard didn't mind because Maddy didn't take him seriously.

His restaurant was better because she was part of it. They came in on days it was closed, made love in every corner of it, and spent hours just lying in each other's arms talking. Later, he would cook for her, and the new dishes she inspired would make it onto the menu the following week. The reviews of his restaurant had never been better. One reviewer said his dish had made love to his taste buds in a way that would forever leave him searching to re-create that pleasure.

Just when Richard thought Maddy could not amaze him further, she invited his mother and his sister to his restaurant to celebrate one particularly good review he'd gotten. His relationship with his mother had always been complex, but Maddy asked him to put that aside long enough to enjoy a meal with her. She asked him to put the past behind him for the sake of his sister. It wasn't until he and his family sat, laughing over old stories long after the restaurant closed, that Richard saw Maddy's a true genius.

She loved completely, unconditionally, and with an almost childlike belief that if a person gave love a chance, it would always prevail. When Richard was with her, his own natural pessimism fell away. He wanted—no, needed—to see the world through her eyes.

Only one thing weighed on him. In all the months that Maddy had lived with him, she hadn't spoken of her family. In fact, it was the only topic that was off limits with them. He'd been beside her when they'd called and heard her come up with excuse after excuse why she was too busy to talk to them. He didn't like to eavesdrop on her conversations, but he'd done so accidentally one or twice and what he'd heard concerned him. She didn't want to go home for a visit. She didn't want her family to visit her.

Richard had gone out and bought an engagement ring for Maddy. It was a single, brilliant solitaire that reminded him of her brilliant smile. He carried it with him, more than ready to propose.

But he held back.

He knew there was something he needed to do first.

✧ ✧ ✧

MADDY STOOD BESIDE Alyson's car and gave Richard's sister a kiss on either cheek. She gathered her bags from the trunk of her car and smiled with satisfaction. They'd spent the day, as they had many times before, hunting down vintage clothing to sell in Alyson's store. The two had laughed their way through trying on many of the outfits and, as usual, Maddy had found a few pieces for herself. She and Alyson had an easy friendship that sometimes made her miss her mother, but she would push those feelings aside—

determined to live in and enjoy only the present.

Not a big problem, since the present was pretty damn amazing.

Alyson leaned back against the passenger side of her car. "So, Maman is coming this weekend. She wants to know if you'd like to meet her newest boyfriend."

Maddy wrinkled her nose. "Didn't we already meet him? He took us on his yacht in the Riviera? Remember, he had that onboard chef who argued with Richard about how long a soufflé should bake?"

Kicking a rock delicately aside, Alyson said, "That one? He's long gone. This one owns very expensive racehorses. I told her I'd go if you did."

Well, that cements it. "If you want me there, Alyson, I'm in. I can't promise not to accidentally call him the wrong name, but I'll try to keep up."

"Richard will come if you do. Thank you for that."

Maddy smiled. "It's wonderful to see all of you together—regardless of who your mother brings along."

"Family is important, *non?*" Alyson asked. "I look forward to seeing yours again when they come. Will they spend the holidays here again? Or will you go home this time?"

Maddy shrugged and adjusted the weight of her bags in her hands. "Well, these are heavy, so I'm going to head in. I'll have Richard call you about this weekend."

Alyson looked like she wanted to say more but didn't. She nodded and waved good-bye. Maddy didn't want to talk about family—not hers, anyway.

Gino rushed forward as if appearing from out of thin air

and took the bags from Maddy's hands. He studied her face for a moment, then said, "You look tired, Maddy. Are you unwell? Would you like me to run to the pharmacy for you?"

Maddy sighed. "Gino, you don't have to carry my bags, and if I'm sick I'll take care of myself. Don't hover over me. You're driving me crazy." *And you're a constant reminder of what I'm trying to forget.*

Gino's expression tightened. "I told your father I would take care of you. I may not have been able to hold you to your promises to him, but I will keep you safe."

"I'm old enough to decide for myself where I will live and who I will live with, Gino," Maddy stormed.

"Which is why Richard's legs are not broken," Gino said blandly. "Still, I don't like that you haven't been honest with your parents. I am loyal to you, Maddy, but you put me in an uncomfortable position by forcing me to also lie. When are you going to tell your family the truth?"

Feeling cornered, Maddy snarled, "They don't deserve the truth. I'll be honest with them when I see them being honest with each other. Don't talk to me about this again, Gino."

Gino's eyebrows rose, but he nodded with offended deference.

Maddy instantly felt awful for snapping at someone who had spent so many years caring for her. "I'm sorry, Gino. Maybe I don't feel well today. I have a headache and I shouldn't have taken it out on you."

"Should I call Richard? You shouldn't be alone if you're ill."

"It's nothing, Gino. Probably too much wine with lunch. I'll have something to eat, then go lie down."

Gino walked her into the house, did his normal sweep to make sure the house was secure, then said he would be nearby if she needed him. Maddy was tempted to tell him once more that he didn't need to worry about her, but it would be like telling the wind not to blow. Gino was the type who would probably stay with her even if her parents never paid him a dollar more for his service. He didn't deserve her impatience.

I'm sorry, Gino.

Maddy stepped out of her suede boots and bent down to pick up the cat that was twirling around her legs. She looked him straight in the eye. "Well, it's me and you until Richard gets home. What do you want to do? Practice verb conjugations with me? I have a test on Friday."

The cat meowed loudly.

Maddy made a *tsk-tsk* sound at him. "Don't judge my language ability, Minet. I don't see you doing any better with it." The cat struggled to get down and Maddy let him go. "See, if you judge others they tend to toss it right back at you. There is a life lesson in there for you."

Thirty minutes later, Maddy was carrying a bowl of soup and a baguette to the kitchen table when she heard the door to the house open. She put the food down, and when she recognized Richard's footsteps, she rushed to him. A passionate romp with him was exactly what she needed to clear her head. She threw her arms around his neck and welcomed him home with a kiss that normally would have had him stripping her clothing off.

Instead, he broke off the kiss and held her back so he could look her over. "Gino said you weren't feeling well."

Maddy started unbuttoning Richard's shirt. "Gino worries too much." She couldn't understand why Richard was still talking when they could be getting naked and enjoying something that involved little to no words.

"He cares about you."

"Forget Gino. Forget everything except this." Maddy kissed Richard's neck and heard him suck in a harsh breath. She didn't want to believe it, but it felt as if he was about to tell her stop. Usually it took nothing more than a look from Maddy for Richard to get so excited he couldn't think of anything besides having her. She told herself she was being paranoid and reached for the clasp of his trousers.

Richard stilled her hands with his. "Maddy, we need to talk."

A wave of embarrassment flooded over Maddy. She'd never been sexually open with anyone, and his words hit her like a rejection. She released his pants angrily. "Talk? Seriously? Right now?" Panic set in. He took a step back from her and frowned. She'd never seen that expression on his face before, and every awful possible reason for it ran through her head. "Oh, my God, what is it? Are *you* sick?"

He shook his head.

"Are you losing your restaurant?"

"Of course not."

"Oh, my God, you're married."

Richard pinched the bridge of his nose and closed his

eyes for a moment before answering. He opened his eyes and said, "This is not about my health, my work, or another woman. This is about us."

Maddy's eyes rounded. "If you don't say it, I may throw up on your feet. That's not a threat, it's a real possibility. Not because I'm sick, but because you're scaring me."

He raised a hand and caressed her cheek. "Please don't, these are new shoes."

She didn't laugh at his joke. The air was pregnant with the promise of bad news. "Just say it. Whatever it is, just get it out there."

He tipped her head up and ran his thumb over her lips. "I love you, Madison Andrade, more than I ever imagined I could love anyone."

"This is how you finally tell me you love me?" She slumped at his words. "That is the worst delivery of those three beautiful words I've ever heard of." She pushed his hand away from her face.

" 'Love' is a word I don't use easily," Richard said, but his tone held a sadness Maddy couldn't understand. "I didn't want to say it until I knew you were the woman I wanted to spend the rest of my life with."

Maddy covered her eyes with her hands and took a deep breath. Her emotions were in a tangled mess. "I'm going to need a minute to absorb this." Although she heard his words, she couldn't ignore what she'd seen in his eyes. She looked up at him, confused. "If this is a proposal, why does it feel like a good-bye?"

Richard didn't deny it, and Maddy's stomach lurched

again. "You're not going to like what I'm going to tell you, but please hear me out."

Maddy turned away. "I don't want to hear whatever you're leading up to. Listen, maybe I should spend the night in town. Maybe you're upset that Gino ended your night at work early. I don't know, but I can guarantee that you should rethink whatever you're about to say."

Richard walked up behind her and laid a hand on her lower back, talking softly into her ear. "There you go, Maddy, running away from what you don't want to see."

She spun on him angrily. "Hey, I'm not the one who just delivered a marriage proposal that sounded like a eulogy."

Richard held her eyes. "I didn't ask you to marry me."

Maddy's chest tightened painfully. "I can see this conversation isn't taking a turn for better."

Richard took both of her arms in his hands and held her before him. "Do you love me, Maddy?"

Angry tears filled Maddy's eyes. "How can you ask that after all this time we've been together? Do you think I would be here if I didn't?"

His hands tightened on her arms. "I don't want to lose you, but you can't stay here with me anymore, Maddy. You need to go home to your family. It's time."

Maddy's knees buckled in shock beneath her. "What are you saying? I don't understand."

He held her against his chest and tucked her beneath his chin. Maddy heard his heart thudding loudly in his chest as he said, "I want you with me because you love me and you don't want to be anywhere else. I don't want you to be here because you don't want to be there. You need to go home, Maddy, and sort things out with your family."

Maddy tore free from his embrace. "Wait, let me get this straight, you love me so much that you're telling me to leave?"

He nodded sadly.

"Will you come with me?" she demanded.

"Non," he said, his expression unreadable. "I would distract you from what you need to address—the reason you came here in the first place."

"I came here because I was sick and tired of the lies. I thought you understood that. But I don't care about them anymore."

"You do. And they stop you . . ."

"What is it that I haven't done, Richard? I thought what we had was perfect. I get along with your family, your friends. I'm learning your damn language. Tell me, which part of this are you not happy with?"

Richard tucked a wild hair behind Maddy's ear. "I am happy. You're not. And you won't be as long as you hide here with me. Go home, Maddy. Face whatever drove you here. And then, if you still want to be here, come back to me."

"Wow, no wonder they say the French are smooth. You make breaking up with me sound like the screenplay for a B-rated chick flick. Let me give you the American version of what you're saying. *It's not you; it's me. I'm not ready for something as wonderful as you.* Only in your speech, you're ending it because *I'm* not ready for *you.*"

"Maddy—"

He reached for her and she smacked his hand away. "No, don't touch me. You want me to leave. I'll leave."

She raced toward the door and opened it. She was halfway down the stairs when Richard caught up to her, swinging her around by the arm. "We're not done with this conversation."

Gino appeared beside them. Ever present. Ever protective. Maddy had never been so happy to see him. "Tell him to let go of my arm, Gino."

Gino stood directly beside them and said, "Richard, I don't want to hurt you."

Richard didn't let go. "I respect you, Gino, but this is between Madison and me."

Gino put his hand over Richard's in warning. "I'm sorry, Richard."

Richard looked from Maddy to Gino's hand and released her. "Maddy, hate me if you want, but I'm right, and I do love you. I hope someday you understand that."

Maddy rushed away from the two of them, stopping only when she reached the street. Gino was beside her in a heartbeat. He said, "My car is across the street."

In a state of shock, Maddy followed him silently. She couldn't believe that Richard didn't want to be with her. She was angry and ashamed of how easily she'd given him her heart. *How could I have been so stupid?* "Take me to the airport," she told Gino.

"Would you like to stop in town for anything?"

Maddy looked back at Richard's house and tears filled

her eyes. “No, everything I care about is in there.” She wiped away a tear and swore. “Shit, Gino, I forgot my purse and my phone in there.”

“I’ll be right back,” Gino said and strode toward the house. He returned a short time later with both.

Not surprising, Maddy thought, *why would Richard hang onto either when he wants me gone?*

Gino started the car and asked, “Where should I tell the pilot we’re going?”

“I don’t care,” Maddy said, watching the French countryside pass in the window. “I officially don’t care about anything anymore.”

Chapter Seven

OF COURSE, GINO took her to her parents' home in New York. Her parents hugged her and kissed her until she pleaded reprieve, blaming jet lag and fatigue for why she wanted to go directly to her room. The truth was she was speaking and interacting on autopilot.

She retreated to her suite of rooms and stayed there well into the next day. Her mother stopped by several times to ask her if she wanted to have breakfast together, go shopping, or simply talk. Maddy declined each time. She closed the heavy curtains in her room, turned off all the lights, and embraced the oblivion of sleep.

There was only one word she could think of to describe how she felt inside: *shattered*.

Her excuses bought her a day alone, but on her second day home her father came into her room, turned on all the lights, and sat on the edge of her bed.

"Your mother is worried about you, Maddy," he said with forced sternness.

Maddy turned away from him, hugging her blankets to her. "I'm fine. I'm just exhausted."

He touched one of her curls lightly. "If you're afraid your mother and I will find out you were living with that Frenchman while you were in Sablet, we already know. Gino is not the only one who watches out for you."

Maddy closed her eyes. "Thanks for trusting me, Dad."

Her father gave a grunt of displeasure. "I shouldn't have to hire people to tell me what my daughter is up to. She shouldn't be lying to me."

"I'm sorry, I didn't realize our family was above lying now."

"You're still angry with me about Stephan?"

"Did Uncle Victor tell him the truth yet?"

Her father remained silent.

"I didn't think so. So, yes, I'm still angry. I tried to put this out of my head while I was in Sablet, but that doesn't mean I'm okay with it. You have no right to play with other people's lives. Letting Stephan think Dominic Corisi stole Isola Santos when, in fact, Uncle Victor asked him to buy it is bad enough. But letting Stephan continue to believe that Nicole had anything to do with Victor losing his company? That's too upsetting for me to live with. Do you understand why I am disgusted when I look at you now? All I can think is that the father I grew up admiring is a hypocrite who doesn't protect his family at all."

Alessandro shifted on the bed beside her and sighed. "Maddy, what Stephan had with Nicole was a summer flirtation. If I honestly thought it was more than that I would agree with you. And, I have spoken to Victor many times about how he should tell Stephan the truth about Isola

Santos. It's not my place to do more than that. Stephan is Victor's son. I can't come between them. Just as Victor would never tell me how to raise you, I cannot interfere with him and his son."

"We're not children anymore, Dad."

"A parent doesn't stop worrying or trying to guide his child just because she reaches a certain age. It was killing me to stay here rather than go to France and haul you home. It wasn't the right place for you, but your mother and I wanted you to come to that decision on your own."

Maddy kept her face averted. "I'm not here because I want to be."

"Making the right choice is not easy, Maddy. You didn't belong in France. Of course you'll miss it for a time, but you'll feel better soon."

Maddy sat up and spun, slapping her hands beside her on the bed. "This is not like the puppy I brought home that you wouldn't let me keep."

Alessandro stood. "No, Richard was not a puppy. He was the first man you cared about. I understand the ways of the heart. I'm not so old that I can't remember the sting of my first breakup. But it passes, Maddy. Don't stay in bed all day making everyone worry about you. It'll only make you feel worse." He stood and started toward the door.

Maddy called out to him. "Dad, I didn't break up with Richard. He said he loved me, then he told me to leave."

Her father slowly turned back in her direction, holding the handle to her bedroom door in one hand.

Maddy clasped her hands on her lap. "He said I had to

sort out things out with my family before I could be with him. Do you think he said that because he never truly loved me and only wanted me to leave?"

Alessandro frowned and shrugged one large shoulder. "I can't speak for him."

"I'm so angry, Dad, but I don't want to be. I don't want to be angry with him. I don't want to be angry with you or Uncle Victor. I want to forget I ever heard what happened between Stephan and Victor, but I can't. So what do I do?"

"Get up. Get showered and come downstairs."

Maddy let out a tearful laugh. "That's it? That's your advice?"

He shrugged again. "Your life is not in this bedroom, Maddy. It's downstairs with the people who love you. No one is perfect. No family is, either. It's time for you to grow up and accept that."

"And Richard?"

"You know how I feel about the French." Alessandro closed the door behind him.

✧ ✧ ✧

A WEEK LATER, Richard was at the restaurant kitchen during a busy dinner rush. He paused while making a sauce to check his phone. Seven days, two hours, and thirty-two minutes ago he had made what felt like the biggest mistake in his life.

It wasn't that he regretted what he'd said. Maddy needed to address her issues with her family. She'd told him enough about them that he knew she wasn't in danger. He never would have sent her back if he'd thought for a second she would be. It brought him comfort to know Gino would give his life for Maddy.

Hard to hate a man like that, even when he cuts a conversation short.

Not that anything I might have said would have made it better.

Idiot. I choose my words as indiscriminately as a dog chooses which ass to sniff.

I should have shown her the ring.

I should have gone back with her when she asked me to.

Bertrand turned off the flame beneath the pan Richard was absently moving back and forth. "Hey, my lovesick friend, try to not to burn every dish, *non?* We still have some patrons."

Richard saw the blackened sauce smoking in the pan he held and swore. "This is unusable. Shit."

Bertrand called the saucier over and the plate Richard had been working on was whisked away. "No worries. Do not be offended, but I've been doubling your orders this week. The lamb that you made was dry enough to make the cats out back gag, but it never left the kitchen."

Richard shook his head in disgust. "I've lost the only woman I've loved and now I've lost my ability to cook."

With a pat on the back, Bertrand led Richard away from the busy part of the kitchen. "Oh, the pangs of love tested. You haven't lost your gift, Richard. The problem is, you cook with your heart. And that sauce, it was dreamt up by a happy man, as was most of what is on the menu now. You have a choice to make, my friend. You can burn every recipe that reminds you of your little American, or you can take all that angst and create something new."

Richard looked down at the pastry ovens his business partner had led him to. "I can't come up with a new recipe now. I can barely concentrate on what I already know how to do."

Bertrand gave him a knowing smile. "Try, Richard. You're an artist. Make something so good that it will bring comfort to someone who feels as badly as you do. I challenge you, Richard, to grow from this."

"I did the right thing," Richard said as he gathered a variety of ingredients. "She would never have been happy without her family."

"You know, those Americans, they think every story needs the same happy ending to be beautiful. What you did for her, Richard, was an unselfish act of love. So make me taste that. Make something so painfully delicious that I cry as I take the last bite because it is over and yet I am better for having tasted it."

A spark lit within Richard and he set out to do just that.

Chapter Eight

THANKSGIVING SNUCK UP on Maddy. She'd followed her father's advice that day and had come down and faced her family, and time had flown by after that. In a family the size of hers, there was always a wedding to prepare for, a birth to celebrate, or someone who needed more cheering. There were members of her family dealing with sick children or cheating spouses, and they needed her. No, she hadn't revealed secrets that weren't hers to tell, but she'd found a way to be okay with them.

She'd taken a job as Stephan's secretary. Working closely with him allowed her to keep track of him, make him smile on days when he was sad, and guide him away from his own anger. They had grown close and although, she didn't feel it made up for her uncle's actions, it was good.

She'd waited for Richard to call her. She'd planned out exactly how to tell him off when he did. But he never called. Eventually, the pain of that, too, became something she accepted and survived.

In a blink of an eye, summer had become fall, and her family was once again gathered at her parents' home. Table after table was put up throughout the house, the number gathered far exceeding what could be contained to one dining room, even though it could easily seat forty.

Children raced through every room, sometimes stealing treats from the tables. Maddy tapped the hand of one she caught sipping from a wine glass. He'd almost started to cry, then ran off when his mother entered the room. This Andrade holiday was a loud, chaotic, and above all loving in a way that Maddy was familiar and comfortable with. She smiled across the table at Stephan. He'd almost wormed his way out of the day, claiming he had work to do, but Maddy had been there to remind him of the importance of family.

Her Uncle Victor clinked his fork against the side of his glass, magically quieting even the youngest of the Andrades. "Thank you, Alessandro, for hosting Thanksgiving for all of us."

Alessandro raised his glass to his brother. Although it was his home, Victor was the older brother, and in their family was something to be honored.

Victor continued. "Thanksgiving is one of my favorite holidays because it reminds us to stop and remember all that we are grateful for. Many look at us and envy our possessions, but our true legacy is all of you."

A baby let out a deafening cry in his mother's arms. She bounced him, trying to comfort him.

Victor waved a hand at the young child. "It's him, and each and every one of us gathered here today. So turn to the person next to you and tell them you are grateful for them. It's the simplest thing to do, but something we often forget."

All around the dining room and in the rooms attached, people stood and hugged. Maddy's eyes filled as she watched. *How did I ever think I could live without this?*

Her mother tapped her on the shoulder and pulled her in for a tight hug. "You will never know how grateful I am for you, Maddy, and happy you came back home to us."

"I'm grateful for you, too, Mom. And everyone else."

As Maddy said it, she realized something she couldn't believe she hadn't before. *Richard sent me home because he knew how much I love my family. He knew I needed to be here.*

"Are you okay, Maddy?" her mother asked.

"I am," Maddy answered. *I'm just finally waking up.* "I have to go, Mom. I'll be right back, but I need to go to my room for a minute."

"Okay, but we're about serve the meal. Be quick."

"I will," Maddy promised and bolted for the privacy of her room. Once inside, she took out her laptop and poured out her thoughts in an email to Richard.

Dear Richard,

When we first met you told me that you were years beyond me when it came to experience. I thought you were wrong. I didn't think I had any more growing up to do.

I was so angry with you when you asked me to leave. I thought I was happy in Sablet. But, I was embracing denial with abandon. I couldn't see that at the time. When you told me to return to my family to mend the rift between us, all I heard was that you didn't love me. I'm sorry I couldn't see past my own insecurities—my own selfish definition of love.

I know you don't celebrate Thanksgiving, but it's a time when we Americans stop and think about everything that we're grateful for. I am spending the day with my parents and more family than I could list here. I wouldn't be here with them if you hadn't pushed me to return.

I am where I belong. Maybe my parents did raise me to be a little bit of a spoiled princess, but I don't take any of that for granted anymore. I know just how lucky I am to be a part of this enormous, insane family.

That doesn't mean I don't love you.

It doesn't mean I don't miss you.

If this email finds you having already moved on to a new relationship, I want you to know that I am genuinely happy for you.

If you want to see me, Richard, I will fly back tomorrow and as often as I can. But I can't live in Sablet with you again. My family needs me, and I've realized now that I need them just as much.

No matter what you answer, or even if you never do, I will always love you, Richard. And I will always be thankful for the time we had together.

Maddy

She hit *send* and burst into tears.

ACROSS THE GLOBE, Richard burned another dish while he read Maddy's email again and again on his phone. *She loves me.* He was tempted to call her, but he didn't yet know what he'd say. Each time he reread her email, he understood that if he wanted to be with her again he would have to move to do it.

He didn't want a weekend here or there with her. He wanted it all—marriage, children, and to be part of that insane, loving family of hers.

And he suddenly knew what he had to do. He called across the kitchen. "Bertrand, you're going to have to run this restaurant without me. I'm going to live in the United States and open a restaurant there."

His business partner smiled. "It's about time."

Epilogue

MADDY ROLLED OVER in bed, having spent half the night naked in the arms of her husband, and decided that Christmas was now officially her favorite holiday. "Are you awake, Richard?"

"Yes," he answered in French before switching to English. "But do I have to be?"

"It's our first Christmas as a married couple. I don't want to miss a moment of it."

He pulled her close and kissed her forehead. "We'll have a lifetime of holidays together. Let me sleep for five more minutes."

"Okay, if you're willing to risk facing my father's wrath if we're late."

"Your father loves me."

"Only because you keep feeding him. No one is going to fit into any of their clothing if you keep bringing desserts to every meal."

"Hey, it was my food that won them over. And your cute speech."

"Cute? You thought I was cute that day? I sounded like a shrew."

"No, you sounded like a woman in love. When you stood up and demanded that everyone love me because you do, I fell in love with you all over again."

Maddy rained kisses on his face until he opened his eyes. "I felt like that when you asked my father for my hand in marriage and then told him you didn't need his money, that your restaurants would support us. It was so old-fashioned, and so romantic."

Richard took both of her hands in one of his and rolled over until she was pinned beneath him. In French, he asked, "Is there no way to silence you, woman?"

"We don't have time, Richard. Your mother and sister are going over to my parents' house early." Maddy tried to sound firm, but she was already weakening.

Once again in French, he whispered in her ear a list of everything he wanted, and Maddy licked her bottom lip in anticipation.

Family was important to Maddy, but hers would survive just fine for another hour or two without her. She had a few things she also wanted for Christmas, and none of them required getting dressed.

The End

Don't miss a release or a sale.
Sign up for my newsletter today.
ruthcardello.com/newsletter

Note to my readers

Recipe for Love is a novella that happens before both my *Legacy Collection* and my *Andrade Series.* It is a wonderful lead in to either. As the youngest of eleven children, I love the Andrade family. I hope you do, as well.

Maid for the Billionaire
Book 1 of the Legacy Collection

Dominic Corisi knew instantly that Abigail Dartley was just the distraction he was looking for, especially since having her took a bit more persuading than he was used to. So when business forces him to fly to China, he decides to take her with him, but on his terms. No promises. No complications. Just sex.

Abby has always been the responsible one. She doesn't believe in taking risks; especially when it comes to men – until she meets Dominic. He's both infuriating and intoxicating, a heady combination. Their trip to China revives a long-forgotten side of Abby, but also reveals a threat to bring down Dominic's company.

With no time to explain her actions, Abby must either influence the outcome of his latest venture and save his company or accept her role as his mistress and leave his fate to chance. Does she love him enough to risk losing him for good?

Come Away with Me
Book 1 of the Andrade Series

Gio Andrade:
Rich, powerful, sexy. A man who thinks he has everything . . . until he meets Julia.

Julia Bennett:
Sweet, spontaneous, and desperate to sell her jewelry line in New York City. She takes a night job as a security guard to pay the rent.

Sparks fly when she mistakes her boss for an intruder.

He can't get her out of his head. She can't find the strength to deny him.

Will lies bring them together, or tear them apart forever?

About the Author

Ruth Cardello hit the New York Times and USA Today Bestsellers Lists for the first time in 2012. Millions of sales later, her books are compared to potato chips; addictive from the first one. Her multi-series billionaire world, with a combination of escapism and realism, has gained her a faithful following of readers.

Ruth was born the youngest of 11 children in a small city in northern Rhode Island. She spent her young adult years traveling and exploring. She lived in Boston, Paris, Orlando, New York then came full circle and moved back to New England. She now happily lives one town over from the one she was born in. For her, family trumped the warmer weather and international scene.

She was an educator for 20 plus years, the last 11 as a kindergarten teacher. When her school district began cutting jobs, Ruth turned a serious eye toward a love she's had for most of her life – writing. She's never been happier.

When she's not writing, you'll find Ruth spending quality time with her children, playing with her two grandbabies, connecting with her readers online, or running around her small farm with her husband, horses, and chickens.

Contact Ruth:
Website: RuthCardello.com
email: ruthcardello@gmail.com
FaceBook: Author Ruth Cardello
Instagram: authorruthcardello
TikTok: @author.ruthcardello
Bookbub: bookbub.com/authors/ruth-cardello

Sign Up for Ruth's Mailing List

ruthcardello.com/signup

One random newsletter subscriber will be chosen every month in 2014. The chosen subscriber will receive a $100 eGift Card! Sign up today by going to the link above!